Bedtime Stories

By Maureen A. McGovern

Title Page

Time Travel with Three Brothers and a Grandma

Malachy, Rafferty and Fergus meet their dad when he was a little boy. They also met their Aunt Colleen and Grandma Mo in the past. In addition, they met their great grandparents in the past.

One Saturday afternoon, the boys were playing at Grandma Mo's house, in the back yard. They have played out there many times in the past and always had fun. Some of their favorite activities in the backyard are kicking the soccer ball around and playing water games. Water games involve playing with the hose and large water guns. If the weather is hot, they can shoot each other with the water guns but if it's cold they must stick with watering bushes and flowers.

But this day was cloudy and that's when the special portal comes to life, if you are lucky enough to locate it through the trees. In Grandma Mo's backyard, special things happen besides the fun of playing back there; the boys know about that. But the magic events can be different each time they happen. The best chance of having a special event is on a cloudy day. In a portal in this backyard, is an area that if one makes contact with it at just the right time, one can time travel. Grandma Mo had a sense that today would be a good day and said to the boys, "Hey, guys, come over. It's going to work today." "Yay, they yelled." Malachy and Rafferty have been curious about meeting their parents when they were children. Today it looks like they will get to meet their daddy when he was a little boy. They stood by their Grandma Mo, all holding hands and Grandma Mo said out loud, "Let us travel to 1524 Akron Drive in the 1980s." Everyone took a deep breath, closed their eyes and as a soft wind blew by, off they went. They had a slight sensation of flying but if felt more like a dream than real.

In a matter of seconds, they landed in the backyard of 1524 Akron Drive, daddy's childhood home. Daddy happened to be in his backyard playing soccer with Aunt Colleen.   Of course they did recognize Grandma Mo; she was their mom but much older than the mom they knew; this seemed a bit unsettling for them.   It also was a bittersweet feeling for Grandma Mo. Grandma Mo asked daddy, Ryan, how old he was. He said he was eight years old and Aunt Colleen was 9 years old.   And so now they knew it was the year 1983. Daddy and aunt Colleen were looking at Grandma Mo curiously, she now was 33 years older than she was in 1983 so she looked similar but different, older and with much grey hair.   The youngest boy wanted to start playing right away and seemed oblivious to the significance of this experience, understandably because he was a toddler. However curiosity took over with the older two brothers and they began talking instead, asking questions faster than they could be answered. Grandma Mo explained to daddy and aunt Colleen that they time traveled and these boys are Ryan's sons and Colleen's nephews; they would all meet up again in the future, starting in the year 2010.   Daddy and Aunt Colleen felt this time travel was very hard to believe but Grandma Mo made a compelling story that convinced them it was true. To verify the truth, Grandma Mo told daddy and aunt colleen a few stories about themselves when they were little; stories only they would know. Then they figured this time travel must be real. One wonders if they will remember this much later in life when they are adults.

Grandma Mo asked boys to each tell their dad something about his future self. Malachy told daddy that one day he would live in a big house with them and their mommy. He also told daddy that mommy likes cats and she knows a lot. Rafferty told daddy that he would take them to the park to play and also take them on long adventure walks. Both brothers told him of the adventures of their younger brother, Fergus, who was a toddler and too young to speak for himself. Daddy was definitely curious about his future as was aunt Colleen about hers. Rafferty told aunt Colleen that she had a husband named Mike and he is a chef. Malachy said when they spend the night at her house, Uncle Mike makes pancakes for them in the morning. Malachy told daddy that he goes to work during the daytime and mommy stays home and plays with them and takes good care of them. Mommy takes them to school. Also, they told daddy that he gets them ready for bed at night with baths, brushing teeth and stories when he tucks them in at night. Malachy said Grandma Mo tells really good bedtime stories and they like it when they stay overnight at her house.

Daddy thought about this for a minute and asked the boys what he looked like as a grown up. Aunt Colleen had the same question about herself. They said that daddy didn't have a lot of hair like he does now and that he's really tall and strong. He can lift them up high in the air and he can carry them on a walk, too. They told aunt Colleen she is very pretty and has long hair. She is really fun and likes to go to the playground with them and also take them on walks. Sometimes the boys spend the night at Aunt Colleen's house and have a really good time playing games, painting, running around outside and drawing.

Now it was time to go inside and see daddy's childhood house. Much to their surprise, their great grandparents were there visiting, Grandpa James and Grandma Alice. Malachy and Rafferty had heard a lot about them but never met them because they passed away before the boys were born. Grandma Alice and Grandpa James told the boys a few stories about their Grandma Mo when she was a little girl. That was fun but the boys were anxious to learn more about their daddy and his life as a boy.

Malachy and Rafferty noticed a large box with a cord hanging on the wall in the kitchen; it was a phone, an old fashioned phone. They have occasionally seen wall phones. Grandma Mo explained that in the 80s, often people would have only one or two phones in their house and they always had cords attached. Sometime later, there were cordless phones and then much later, cell / mobile phones as is usual today.

Mostly, the boys wanted to see daddy's room. The brothers were very surprised at how small daddy's rooms is. Also, they noticed his room was fairly organized and clean. This was quite different from their own rooms. Daddy had a bed, desk and dresser and a small closet in his room. They wanted to know about the kind of toys daddy had in his room, with special interest in star wars paraphernalia. Daddy didn't have too many toys, mostly gear to play outside and a few random toys and books; by today's standards his room appeared minimalistic. On daddy's dresser was a trophy for baseball. In the garage they found a bicycle, soccer goal and bicycle.

They asked to see Aunt Colleen's room. Aunt Colleen also had a bed, dresser, desk and small closet in her room. She also had some dolls and stuffed animals as well as various other personal items. Colleen's room looked cozier than Ryan's.

For more information about the environment, Ryan and Colleen took the boys to the basement and garage. In the basement were many cabinets and shelves for storage. The washing machine and dryer were downstairs, too. There was a large area with a big carpet on the floor and a couch and chair. Sometimes Colleen and Ryan went to the basement to play or read. In the event of a tornado or bad storm, the basement was a comfortable and safe place to go. The garage held lawn equipment, bicycles, and sporting equipment. There was barely room to put a car. It was a single car garage. Everything was much smaller than what the boys are used to today, the house, bedrooms, garage. Everything except the yard. The back yard was big with plenty of room to set up goals for soccer and bases for baseball. It was a very good yard for growing up years. Daddy and Aunt Colleen had some very fun times in the back yard.

The boys also met the family dog, Duke. He was a mixed breed, mostly german shepherd. Duke was friendly and maintained the disposition of a puppy for most of his 14 year life.

Grandma Mo said they would have just a short time to stay because they must return to the current day soon. She encouraged each boy to ask daddy, aunt Colleen or the great grandparents a question about their lives. So they thought about it and asked several questions. Malachy asked daddy what his school is like and who his friends are; he asked Aunt Colleen the same question. Rafferty asks daddy and Aunt Colleen about what their favorite games are and who they play with.

Grandma Mo said it was time to go. The boys asked when they could return and how old would daddy be when they return. Of course nobody knows that answer. They also wanted to know about mommy when she was young. Where is she and can they see her? Daddy said he doesn't know her yet. Grandma Mo said that mommy and daddy didn't know each other for many, many years to come. She didn't live in that neighborhood and it will be some time before they meet. They all said their goodbyes. Daddy and Aunt Colleen said they will be very excited to meet the boys again. Grandma Mo said her goodbyes and took Fergus in tow. Off they went back to 2016.

The Pastels Part 1 (Part 2 coming soon)

Jack and Merri Pastel live in a three story house in an urban neighborhood in the middle of America. They love their neighborhood; this is where they raised their children. They have lived many years here and have both happy and sad memories, mostly happy. Now they are old and their children and grandchildren live far away. Their days are quieter than in younger years and slower.   They take tai chi class together once a week and go on short walks in the neighborhood. Most days Jack and Merri enjoy their lives and especially like living in their special house.   Jack enjoys finding good stories on the internet and creating short movies for fun. He still enjoys drawing, too.   Merri enjoys knitting shawls, mittens, hats and scarfs, as well as painting beautiful scenes on canvas. Jack and Merri have a cozy studio with easels for their drawing and painting efforts. They stay in close touch with their kids and grandkids through phone, texting and their favorite - facetime. They love being able to see the childrens' faces as they are speaking. The kids show their artwork and their toys so Jack and Merri know their current interests.

The house of Jack and Merri is an old one with very high ceilings and long windows. One of their favorite parts of the house is a big screened in porch in the back, off the kitchen. In fact, they can often be found there reading a book, listening to music, or just chatting. It's a peaceful and private area. Other aspects of the house include a large living room and dining room. These areas are comfortable enough to entertain and not be crowded. The kitchen is roomy with lots of old cabinets and a tall pantry. In the kitchen is a dumb waiter. A dumb waiter is a platform with a pulley on it and one can transport materials from the first floor to the second or third and back down again by way of pulling the ropes. The dumb waiter is located inside what looks like a closet or cabinet; it's big enough for a small adult to sit in and ride up and down. Usually it's used to move something of an awkward shape or heavy weight as to avoid taking it up the stairs. The dumb waiter is a special feature of the house. Remember this. Keep in mind that Jack is an architect. He especially liked adding special features to a house. Now this house had some other special features. For one thing, all the bedrooms were on the second floor, and a couple bathrooms too. This makes it nice for when their kids visit; everyone is comfortable and no one is too crowded. Something else is interesting   From the first to the second floor there are two staircases; this was typical in older houses. One staircase was in the front of the house; it was grand with beautiful spindles and a lovely curve creating a striking appearance. The other staircase was built in the back of the house, off the kitchen. It was plain, simple and fairly steep. This was originally the staircase for the servants and in the very old days, people didn't seem to care about the quality of the servants' lives. Another story for another time.   Usually in the case of a third floor, only one staircase was needed. However while a regular staircase is not evident, there is a secret staircase going from the second floor to the third floor. Jack and Merri seemingly only used the first and second floors of their house. When their kids were growing up, they were never allowed to attempt to go to the third floor. Nobody ever knew what was on the third floor. Maybe we'll find out later in the story.

Don't forget about the basement. In very old houses, the basement usually has a low ceiling. Often the floor is made on cement and sometimes the floors consist of dirt or gravel. In this case, the floor is cement, grey cement. The ceiling is low; Jack has to duck when he walks in the basement and Merrie just barely can stand up without ducking. The basement has a few super small windows so it tends to be rather dark and gloomy down there. Things you will find in the basement include the furnace, hot water heater, humidifier, washer and dryer. There are also shelves which contain many boxes of Christmas, Easter, Halloween, Thanksgiving and birthday decorations and lots of childhood books and toys that the kids used long ago. There are a few bicycles, roller skates, shovels, random cans of paint and boxes of tools. Of course there is a workbench. The workbench has some tools attached and a pegboard on the wall with various tools hanging from pegs. The workbench is the place to go if you want to build or repair something. Jack and Merri don't go in the basement much anymore. They might go down there to look for something special but they aren't building or repairing too much these days. Basements can be scary, especially when they are dark. In this basement, there is a small room with stone walls and a big metal plate on the wall leading to the outside.This room is all black; it's called the coal room. There's nothing in it anymore, at least I don't think there is but it's pitch black so I don't really know. Back in the old days, houses were heated with coal. Once a week a coal man would come by with a large truck of coal and shovel coal into the window where the metal plate is. When Jack and Merri needed coal for heat , they would go to the basement and fill up a bucket, take that upstairs to the fireplace and light the fire.

Usually for Christmas the children, Rosemary, Tom, and Judy, visit with their children. There is plenty of room for everyone to stay in this big, rambling house with many bedrooms. The siblings always love getting together in their parents' house every year they have fun catching up with each other and getting to know each other's families better.

In younger years, Merri was a teacher in an elementary school. She taught students and later their children and sometimes even their grandchildren. The school was at the center of the community and everyone knew each other. Jack was an architect and designed houses and remodeled houses for people who wanted to add on to their homes or have a special feature. Jack especially enjoyed designing special features in a house, such as a distinctive space with a higher or lower ceiling and hidden rooms. Remember this. People usually used hidden rooms for storage. More than once, Jack built special reading rooms, designed by Merri, with lighting and shelves for books as well as built in benches and lounge areas. Jack can look at the outside of a house and describe the floor plan. Jack and Merri are retired from their professional jobs and now have available time to do things they couldn't do when working. . Jack and Merri are old but still in good enough condition to live active and fulfilling lives, which is why they are able to visit their grandchildren several times a year.

The street where they live is called Cherry Blossom Street, named after its native Cherry Blossom trees which line the streets forming a canopy over the street. The street is very peaceful and beautiful with the Cherry Blossoms as well as many variou other types of trees, bushes and flowers. The greenery complement the red brick, stone houses and wooden fences.

Every summer, there is a block party and everyone gathers with games, their families and food to share. On Halloween night, there is a firepit with a healthy fire outside on the sidewalk in front of the Pastel's house. Friends and neighbors gather there with food, drinks, treats and lawn chairs. Grown ups talk and catch up on events and news of various family members who have moved away. Children go trick or treating with their bags being filled with candy. Children and adults are dressed in costumes and enjoy guessing who is who behind each mask.   Winter brings everyone outside shoveling driveways and building snowmen. Spring is a good time to catch up with neighbors while tending to their yards and gardens. Summer is when kids are off school and outside playing; it's fun to hear their play even from inside the house. Labor Day festivities bring folks out to visit, marking the end of summer.

Jack and Merri know many of their neighbors, although some of them are new to the neighborhood and haven't yet met. They hold the status of being the parents and / or grandparents of the neighborhood. They have known all the families who moved into the neighborhood, moved out, babies who entered the world and others who left this world. They remember when trees were new and small and there wasn't too much shade in the yards. Now the yards all have beautiful old trees and lawns that provide much shade in the summer and beauty all year, even in the winter. Trees provide nice homes for the birds and squirrels and fun places for children to climb

Jack and .Some neighbors built tree houses for their kids. The treehouse Jack built was the most elaborate treehouse on the block, in the whole neighborhood. His treehouse had three rooms with a hammock, bench with storage and a lid, lights and running water. Every kid in the neighborhood loved playing in that treehouse. Jack built a ladder on the tree for children to climb up and down safely. This playhouse is cool enough that even Jack went up there once in a while for some quiet time, long after the kids were grown up and moved out of the house. There were two ways of getting into the treehouse - a front door and a back door. The front door had the ladder going to the entrance. But the back door had a bridge going to the third floor window of the house. That entrance was well hidden within the many branches of the very large, old tree. In fact from the ground looking up, the bridge to the window is completely hidden. Jack is the only one who knows about it. Do you think he told Merri? What do you think he uses it for?

A Walk in the Snow - Part 1

Back in the 1950s many things were different than today. For example, there was a lot of snow and it was frequent in St. Louis in the 1950s. In 2016, snow is less in volume and frequency. Also today the expectation of possibly one inch of snow could easily get one a school day (a day off school). My guess is that today 3 -5 inches might get you 3 - 5 snoe days. This is due to many factors: there are more vehicles on the streets today, thus making for traffic problems in inclement weather, children from a low socio economic environment may not have proper attire for this weather and they might not have a babysitter if they aren't in school. Due to overall cultural changes in society, children are more dependent on adults today than in the past. In the 50s, one would walk home in less than appropriate attire whether it was healthy or not. Today's adults are more safety conscious than in the past. In the 1950s, if school chose to cancel school early, they simply opened the doors and set the children free. Today, if a school must cancel early, they make automatic phone calls to parents as well as announce it on TV, the radio and publish the information on their web site. Every effort is made to inform parents. Students are kept behind if they don't have confirmation of a place to go. School will provide shelter until parents are contacted and arrangements are made to pick up children.

One cloudy day, around 1957, about 2:00pm snow started falling from the sky. It was the kind of snow that produced very large and wet snowflakes. Because it was already very cold outside, the snow covered the ground very quickly. Looking out the window from my first grade classroom brought an air of excitement. With a snow such as this one, we were very likely to get some time off of school, at least one day. Keep in mind, the weather forecasters in those days did not have access to the same equipment today's' forecasters have, thus thwarting their ability to forewarn schools that a storm was on the way. We simply didn't know until it arrived.

Watching the storm through the windows was fun but what I and everyone else wanted to do was go outside and play in the snow. It was fun to imagine the building of snowmen and sledding opportunities that may be soon available to us and much more than a daydream. It was fun to think about just walking home.

My brother, Mike, and myself walked to and from school every day. As an adult, I believe this is a very good way for kids and adults to begin the day and on the way, one can relax and unwind from the day while walking home. Today very few kids walk to school. Parents and school authorities tend to err on the safe side with kids, that translates to being over protective. The philosophy with some today is why let the kids walk when we can drive them around? It's no accident children are becoming less active.

I am one of four siblings. Growing up, it was standard operating procedures to share clothes and to wear hand me downs. Surely today's children do the same in many cases but it does appear that people today aren't as willing to sacrifice; everything is purchased new and often. Quite often, back in the fifties, most families had only one vehicle because the dad went to work with the car and the mom was home. That particular family model still exists but most families have mom and dad working and two cars. In fact, even if mom or dad stays home with the children, usually every adult has their own car.   That's just how it's done.

    This year for school, I was sporting the absolute cutest pair of little red boots with a graphic, maybe cowgirls, I don't recall. These were rubber boots to be worn over shoes. The only problem with my boots that day, was the fact that the boots were too big. I'm guessing I begged my mom to wear them anyway because they were so cute. To this day, I still love red boots and shoes; I can't resist them. Apparently my shoes were a bit on the large side, too. Here's what happened.

    The snow fell hard and the school authorities decided to send all of us home. As was the case with most classmates, there was no person to pick them up. We all had to walk home. Walking home in deep, heavy snow with boots too big, was a hard task for a little girl. My house was probably about a mile to a mile and a quarter from the school. That isn't too far for kids to walk; it's very quick. But on this day, we noticed the houses all looked the same, snow covered. We also noticed the streets were emptying out due to the people moving faster than us. Bigger kids had an easier time of it. Many kids lived in different directions or lived closer to school than we did. So it was taking us a long time to get home. Of course we didn't have a cell phone to call mom and tell her where we were; that's a very different situation than today's accessibility to communication tools.

    I was cold and starting to get scared because the streets were empty and quiet. But Mike said we could get home if we just kept walking. He took my hand and off we trudged. We managed to get about half way home when as I pulled my foot up to take a step over the snow, I noticed my boot was missing from my right foot, and my shoe. The snow was so deep, it traveled into my boots and became heavy.   For some reason, my sock was still on and very wet. My foot was numb from the cold and that's why I didn't know the boot was off. The snow was so deep that it was hard to walk; I had to pick my knees up almost to my chest with every step just to get through the snow.   We looked around for my boot and thought we would be able to notice it because it was red. I didn't know how long it had been off my foot or how far back on the street it would be. It was too cold, wet, and cloudy to spend very much time looking for the boot. Visibility was impaired because of the rapid rate at which snow was falling. Now we didn't know what to do.

    We hoped for a car to drive by to flag them down for help. Chances are any cars driving by would be driven by a mom or dad of someone in the neighborhood and they would be able to drive us home. But the snow was deeper now, making it harder for cars to drive at all, which is why we weren't seeing any more cars drive by. We decided to walk across a main street, Cameron, and then find a house that we would feel comfortable knocking on its door. That is what we did. We walked the length of two houses, then crossed the street. Now we were on our own street, Estridge. Our next plan was to figure out which house to approach for help. Estridge is a long street and we were at the end of the street where we didn't know the people. But my foot is not getting any warmer or dryer and I still don't have a shoe or boot. We stood in the street looking at four different house and trying to choose one to approach. We noticed one of the houses had footprints in the snow and they looked like small feet. Of course this indicated there was at least one child who lived there. That was the house we wanted.

We approached the door and knocked loudly, waiting patiently on the porch for a response. No answer. Maybe knocking with mittens and gloves wasn't loud enough. We rang the doorbell next. Again no answer. In spite of the cold, we took off our mittens and gloves and knocked on the door louder this time. Now we heard footsteps and became excited and anxious to get the help we so desperately need. Mrs. Applebottom opened the door and asked if she could help us. She is an elderly lady who looks much the same age as both of our grandmas, which is very old. Interestingly enough, that's something else that seems different today, the appearance of grandparents. In the fifties and sixties and even seventies, the grandmas mostly looked old and dressed in certain grandma dresses. There was no mistaking their age range - old. Today's grandmas wear whatever clothes they want and none of them wear grandma dresses. Mrs. Applebottom was wearing the grandma dress and shoes and she had the grandma hair so she was either a grandma or a grandma type. At first appearance, we thought this was the right house to approach for help because we found a grandma type and of course we all know these types can be trusted to help a child in any way needed. Not only that but the grandma type would go to great lengths to make certain a child was not only safe and healthy but also comfortable and happy. All the while, my feet were still wet and cold, my right foot still numb. I was about to start telling her of our situation when Mike began to speak for us both. As the older brother, he felt it was his responsibility to do the talking. Mainly, he wanted to use the phone to call our mom and tell her what was happening with us.

As Mike was speaking, I was taking in everything around us including Mrs. Applebottom who was wearing an apron and smelling of freshly baked cookies. There were two glasses of milk and two small plates of cookies on her kitchen table.

A Walk in the Snow - Part 2

My eyes became very large with wonder which turned to confusion then panic and finally fear. All this happened in a split second but felt like many hours. There were no other kids around and no other adults around so why did Mrs. Applebottom have the table set for two people to have milk and cookies? Did she somehow know we were coming? How could that even be possible? We didn't know which house we were going to until the very last minute when we decided, standing cold in the middle of the snow packed street. How could she have known? Or did Mrs. Applebottom expect two different kids who never showed up? What was going to happen to the milk and cookies if we didn't show up there?

In the meantime, I'm still cold. My foot now is needing some attention but I'm getting more and more afraid. I just want us to be home with our mom. That's not happening now because we can't call our mom and there's no way for her to know where we are. So Mike is asking about using the phone and I am getting more scared looking at the table. Mrs. Applebottom says we'll talk about the phone after we have a sit down at the table and enjoy our milk and cookies like a good little girl and boy.

Mike said it wouldn't hurt to have a little snack before calling mom so I agreed and we both found our seats at the table. In hindsight, I believe Mike was tired and hungry from the walk in the snow; it was a very hard walk for little kids and took an extremely long time. Mike was willing to delay the foot recovery situation as well as being rescued from Mrs. Applebottom's grip. He figured, after we have the snack we can use the phone and our mom would be there very quickly to pick us up and take us to our warm and dry home with the rest of our family.

As we took our seats at the table, Mrs. Applebottom guided me to a seat with a pan of warm water below and instructed me to put my foot right into that pan. It felt strange at first but I left my foot in the warm water while I had my milk and cookies. It was just the right thing to do because the feeling returned to my foot and I felt a sense of relief with a normal feeling foot. Mrs. Applebottom dried my foot with a bath towel and then wrapped a warm blanket around both feet - without socks or shoes. It felt very comfortable.

Mike asked again if we could use the phone to call our mom and Mrs. Applebottom replied neither yes or no but instead suggested we move over to couch and get comfortable first. So we went over to the couch; it was soft and positioned in front of a fireplace with a hot fire burning. We both fell fast asleep within a few minutes while we were waiting to use the phone. When we woke up after a long nap, it was dark and long past dinner time. By now we were more than anxious to get home. Our parents must be very worried about our safety.

Again, Mike asked to use the phone. This time Mrs. Applebottom spoke in a funny voice, different from before. She said, "Foolish little boy, you won't be using the phone. You're with me now and you won't be going home. Same with you, little girl. Ba ha ha."

Her voice was scary and her words terrifying. What in the world is this all about? Every grown up we've ever met has behaved like our parents, being helpful and friendly and making us feel safe and secure. Mrs. Applebottom is acting exactly the opposite. She also seemed to have two different voices; one was a regular, nice lady's voice but the other voice was harsh, high pitched and scary. It was threatening and edgy. This was puzzling to us because all the people we ever met only had one voice each - adults and kids. Maybe she was playing some weird type of game. So I said, "Are we playing a game, Mrs. Applebottom?" "A game of pretend?"

"Ba ha ha ha. Sure we are little girl. Call it what you will. Sure we're playing a game," said Mrs. Applebottom.

By her tone, I could tell that Mrs. Applebottom was not really playing a game and if she was, it was not a safe or fun game, not one we would want to play.

"No you"re not, Mrs. Applebottom. We want to call our mom; let us use the phone," I yelled to Mrs. Applebottom. Mike is being quiet as he's tired, confused and trying to create an escape plan. Mike knows Mrs. Applebottom is not about to help us.

"Ba ha ha ha ha. You little fools. You're with me now. You won't be going home. Hush now," cackled Mrs. Applebottom.

Mike said that we will get out on our own to go home by ourselves. Mrs. Applebottom reminded him that it's now dark out, there's more snow on the ground than when they came to her house and little sister is still missing one shoe and a boot. She can't walk through the snow again, especially in the dark.

I pleaded, "Mrs. Applebottom, please let us use your phone or you call someone to help us. We need to get home. It's so late now and our parents will be so worried about us. They will probably have already called the police. Some of our neighbors might even be walking door to door looking for us."

"That is not a problem little girl. Anybody looking for you will not find you here. Remember, you're with me now. Ba ha ha ha. I have a nice spot for you in my secret room. You'll have a kitchen, bathroom and bedroom there. No one will find you," Mrs. Applebottom threatened.

Come now to your room, boy and girl. Maureen noticed Mrs. Applebottom referred to them as boy and girl rather than using their real names, Mike and Maureen. It was a curious way for an adult to interact with a child. Mike and Maureen followed Mrs. Applebottom to the back of the house, behind the kitchen. She opened a hidden door, which looked like part of a wall, and we walked into a very comfortable big room. It was warm and had a fireplace, bathroom, small kitchen, table and chairs, two beds a couch and a bookshelf. No phone. No window. No outside door.

The idea of living under Mrs. Applebottom's thumb for the rest of our lives was not an idea we relished. I think it would be like living in jail, except probably more comfortable. We wanted to go home to our own family, to our own house, our own beds. Who could blame us? Mrs. Applebottom is not thinking clearly. She behaves nicely at times, bringing us food and caring for my foot but other times she talks about holding us in the house against our will and she talks in that harsh, scary voice. That voice would scare anyone, even grown ups. And she won't let us go to church either. How will we see our friends? This situation is not going to work for us. We must do something and fast.

Mrs. Applebottom said it was time for us to go to bed. We were relieved because now we could formulate a plan of escape without her there. Mike's idea was to go along with Mrs. Applebottom. This way, maybe she would let down her guard and we could get her to leave us alone for a short period while she goes to the store. Then we could use the phone or just escape from the house. I agreed that this could work so we decided to go to bed and then tomorrow morning, we would take on this pretense of wanting to stay there with Mrs. Applebottom.

It was a long night. We were both scared but also very tired and really could not wait until morning time. So we drifted off to sleep. The next morning it had stopped snowing but the accumulated snow was about 2 feet; that's a very tall snow for little kids to walk through. Mrs. Applebottom served us breakfast and we were so hungry we didn't care what kind of food she served us. It happens she served us hot chocolate and oatmeal with raisins. This happened to be a fairly decent breakfast. Afterwards, we asked her if she had any children's' books or games we could play. We noticed she was talking in a normal voice, not the harsh, scary one. Mrs. Applebottom seemed very happy that we asked about books and games. She felt this meant we were getting used to her and her place. Our plan was working.

We both felt sad because we missed our family. We also didn't like the fact that we couldn't look out a window and see what was going on outside. But our plan was to be very thoughtful and patient and catch Applebottom off guard. We had to work the plan.

Mrs. Applebottom brought us a deck of cards, Monopoly, Candyland, paper, colored pencils, crayons and books. She said we have a nice big table to play games on and color and draw. As she left the room to leave us to our play, she said (in a normal voice), "It's so nice to have you back, Tom and Mary." Tom and Mary? What ever is she talking about? Rather, who ever is she talking about? Before this, Ol Applebottom called us boy and girl. Actually, she called us foolish boy and girl.

It's evident Ol Applebottom thinks we are two kids called Tom and Mary. We don't know why she thinks this but she never asked us our names. She had two places set at her table with milk and cookies, as if she was expecting two kids. It looks like we have become part of a strange mystery. Can you guess how we will be able to escape?

The Night of Malachy's Birth

This story tells about the day and night of my first grandchild's birth, told from my perspective. Of course this story told from the perspective of the mom, dad, aunt, or other grandparents would be a different story altogether. Bear with me; as this is my first experience as a grandma.

My son and his wife were expecting their first child the first week of December. Due to potential complications, the doctor advised a date about three weeks prior to the due date to have the baby. The hope is that the baby will decide to arrive at a date three weeks prior to his due date. The baby will risk not getting enough nutrients if he is allowed to go to the end of that three weeks before being born. So if mom doesn't go into labor after a bit of prompting, then the doctor will perform a cesarian operation to help this baby into the world.

During the time surrounding the expected due date, I was working part time. This happened to be my first school year as a retired full time teacher, of thirty years. It happens I found a charter school where I could do some effective work as a Reading Specialist. As it was with that job, I worked three days per week and I was allowed to set my own schedule, for the most part. So, the principal knew that I might need a bit of flexibility around the due date of my grandson. Of course I know that I wasn't needed for any reason; I certainly didn't need to take a day off work for the birth of Malachy. But somehow I had a strong desire to be present. So I made sure my flexible schedule would accommodate this time off work, just for a day; it wasn't difficult to accomplish.

It was scheduled for Meghan to check in to the hospital on Thursday morning. The plan was for her to receive some motivation to begin labor and if she didn't then labor could be induced and / or a cesarean section could be performed. Most importantly, the baby must be rescued in order that he could safely receive proper nutrition. Meghan and Ryan checked in to the hospital at about nine in the morning. Preliminary findings were that she would be monitored and very likely this baby wouldn't be born until very late that night or early the next morning. Grandparents were alerted to relax and not come to the hospital until called. It was going to be a long day for the young parents.

I went about my day with feelings of happiness and excitement for this child to join us. The out of town paternal Grandpa started making his way to St. Louis, planning to arrive in time for the birth, probably early; he had a four to five hour car drive ahead of him. And Meghan's parents were of course prepared to get to the hospital at any given moment. They may have visited her there while she was waiting for labor to begin.

Some time around one or two in the afternoon, Grandpa arrived in St. Louis; he lives in Kansas City, Missouri so he left early in the morning. Soon to be Aunt Colleen picked up her dad from his hotel when he arrived and met me at the hotel restaurant for a bite to eat and conversation while awaiting Malachy. We chatted for a little while at a place close to the hospital so we could get there quickly if needed. Ryan, soon to be a dad, called and said Meghan was resting in the hospital and the doctors were not expecting anything to happen for many hours so he planned to come over and have a bite to eat with us while she rested. For about an hour, we all relaxed and ate lunch, feeling a sense of joy and anticipation waving over us the whole time. I even think I felt butterflies from time to time. We thought we would head back home or hotel to rest then meet up later to visit, have a drink and dinner and generally hold vigil. That was the plan anyway.

About three pm Ryan received a call saying unexpected activity was beginning; Meghan was starting labor. Malachy decided he was on his way. It's very early yet and is still expected to be many hours before he arrives; it's just that Meghan responded to the treatment much sooner than is usual. Ryan promptly returned to the hospital, leaving us with instructions to stay put until further notice. This was not a time a family crowd was needed at the hospital. Now we wait and wait and wait. But that's ok because we expected this. Babies come when they are ready, not necessarily when the family is ready. If babies came when moms were ready, pregnancy would be a much shorter time period than nine months.

So Colleen, Pat and myself stuck around in the restaurant for a while; all of our regular activities were now on hold until Malachy decided to join us. With the knowledge that we could well be up all night long waiting, we decided to go home now; go our separate ways and possibly rest or nap. This turned out to be an excellent idea.

As I was at home, I decided that I would try to go to sleep early in case I got a call in the middle of the night and had to jump up and get to the hospital. At this point we thought Malachy might not join us until the next morning. I was winding down and getting ready for bed; it was around 9:30 in the evening. Definitely too early for bed but if only I could try to drift off into sleep maybe it would work. Then the phone rang. Ryan had news; Malachy was going to be coming along very quickly now. In fact, I thought it entirely possible that the baby would be born before our arrival. Colleen and Pat arrived at the hospital about the same time as I did. Kathleen and John, Meghan's parents, were already there in the lobby outside the maternity ward. What we knew so far was that Meghan was well and the baby was well and wanting to join us a little quicker than previously expected.

Everyone greeted each other. Kathleen gave us the progress report. At this time, we expected Ryan to come down a long hallway that we could see through the vertical glass windows in the doors to the birthing area of the hospital. We awaited his news of this new baby who would soon brighten up our lives. So we talked and walked around; we were the only family in the waiting area at this time. I don't remember ever sitting down, although there was plenty of seating and it looked comfortable enough. But pacing and talking and the sheer excitement of this life changing event prevented the thought of sitting casually and waiting.

They said it would be fast but time is passing and passing. It's now about 10:30 and no update. Occasionally a medical person would enter or exit the doors we were flanking and we asked about getting updates. Everyone was polite and understanding of our anxiety but none of them had answers. They all said we would hear something soon. About eleven pm, a medical person came out and told us that there had been some difficulty with the birth. They didn't know the details of it but that was the reason Ryan hadn't been out to update us; he was by Meghan's side throughout. She told us that it would probably be about forty five minutes to an hour and someone would be out at that time.

Of course we were filled with worry and anxiety. There are so many things that can create difficulty during birth but we only could imagine as we had no information. We prayed for Meghan and the baby, prayed for good health for Meghan and Malachy. We talked but didn't really verbalize any speculations about what was happening. And we watched. We watched fiercely through that window. In fact we noticed the medical folks were now entering and exiting via a different door down the hallway to avoid us. They knew we couldn't help but to ask them for updates and they felt our anxiety.

Finally we saw Ryan come out of a room down a very long hallway. He was too far to be able to read his face but I could tell by the normalcy of his walk that everything was ok. Every step he took seemed like slow motion to me. Teary eyes plagues us all; the emotion was overwhelming. Ryan opened the door and stepped into the lobby with us. He told us what happened. As Malachy was attempting his journey out into the world, the umbilical cord became wrapped around his neck. If it would have happened sooner, the doctors would have done a cesarean section. However, it was too late for that. A team of doctors convened upon Meghan and quickly came to consensus on whether to use forceps or suction. They agreed on forceps and safely rescued Malachy in time to save his life. This was a painful experience for Meghan and she was given strong pain medication.

Ryan said we would wait for a signal from the room and we could all go down to see Meghan and meet Malachy. Very soon came the signal and we entered the room. Meghan was clearly in a dazed state but looked very happy to have this new addition to her family. We watched as the nurses had Malachy on a table and were checking him over. He wasn't in great shape when born but his color and reflexes improved quickly. We are all very fortunate that he survived this life threatening birth. Meghan was going to take some time to recover and would be uncomfortable for a while but she would be ok. After we had clearance from the nurse, Ryan let each of us hold Malachy for a short while. He told us about the birth and the story was overwhelming. I felt so blessed to be there and to have this new life as part of our family.

It was midnight now and time to leave the new family to rest. Kathleen, John, Colleen, Pat and myself went to O'Connell's Pub, right down the street. We drank a lot.

I don't remember if we ate. We were joyous and celebrated and stayed in the bar until they booted us out, about three am. Welcome to the family, Malachy.

Girl Meets Bear

This really happened and I lived to tell about it.

When I was ten years old, my family took a road trip to Yellowstone National Park to have a camping vacation and meet with our Schulein cousins. Mom, Dad, four kids and a station wagon filled with lots of camping equipment, food, water and games. You can imagine a long road trip with four kids would be tough without games.

Preparing for vacation camping trips was always lots of fun, especially planning on which clothes to pack. Usually every summer we got some new clothes. I mostly remember getting some matching shorts sets. Of course when camping one also needs some warmer clothes as well. It must be planned out in advance: swimming clothes and gear, shorts and shirts, at least one nice dress and dress shoes for church, a couple pair of tennis shoes and even a pair of flip flops. My mom was not in favor of flip flops which was ok with me because I always found them uncomfortable. But she always insisted we needed to wear them in showers to prevent picking up athlete's foot. I didn't know what athlete's foot was but I figured it was a disease. I even loved putting together my personal items in a ditty bag. This year for the trip my mom made each of us a ditty bag (a small bag that held our hair and personal hygiene products) with a color coded ribbon featured at the top of this drawstring bag. All of the ditty bags were made of the same fabric, had the same thick, soft rope as the drawstring, and were the same size; we were able to quickly note which was ours by the colored ribbon at the top of the bag; mine was a pretty shade of pink. The color matched our specially made beach towel. I loved the beach towels; they were much better than the ones you could buy in the store because they were thicker and square rather than rectangular. Reminiscing as an adult, I'm surprised a ten year old was so excited about fabric, towels and bags but I was.

The anticipation of the trip was exciting. Each year we went on a long camping trip for about three weeks; we all loved it. We traveled throughout much of the United States and saw much beauty and many places we would not have seen had we opted for the staycation.

Part of the fun for us kids was the car ride. It doesn't seem like it would be that much fun to be cooped up in a car for hours in a day but we always knew we would see some fascinating and very different sights along the way to our destination. Usually we had multiple destinations. Back in those days of long ago, we didn't have seat belts, at least not in the back seats. But I don't recall seeing any seat belts in the front either. Kids didn't sit in the front at all. My mom had a stash of important materials up front - maps, food, and a paddle. If kids misbehaved repeatedly, our mom would hold the paddle and threaten to use it on us. I'm not sure if that ever happened but we believed her and knew if the paddle made an appearance, we better start behaving well. As I remember, three of us sat in the back seat and one of us sat way back in the third seat, the one facing backwards; I'm pretty sure that seat was reserved for my little sister,

Rosemary. I don't know why she would be back there but having a whole seat to yourself could be a good thing. One could stretch out and take a nap if one wanted to. The middle seat was big enough for four of us to sit but there was probably a tendency for rambunctious type behavior in that situation. We could sit on the floor, stretch out on the seat; we always had pillows and could make ourselves pretty comfortable in just about any position seat or floor. The floor was fun to sit on if you wanted to play with dolls or color but you couldn't see out the window. Looking out the window could be very entertaining most of the time but it was best to mix up the seating arrangements so as not to get bored. Now I usually took off my shoes but had them at close reach because if we stopped, I wanted to be able to jump out of the car as fast as possible. Why? I don't know. It just seemed like a good idea. Sometimes, if it was really hot, our parents let us get a bottle of soda from a machine at a gas station. We had to drink it there and then return the bottle right away. I liked it because we were able to drink out of cold, glass bottles. Of course I know that water would have quenched our thirst better than soda but it sure was good. Funny, it's been decades since I drank any type of soda in any type of bottle and I sure don't miss it a bit. But I have fond memories of our vacation sodas.

Packing the clothes, personal belongings, favorite toys and books and games was all part of the anticipation that created excitement. The parents had the more challenging job of planning the final destination and all the stops in between, planning for extra time to be spent in certain places that we liked more than others, planning for the unexpected. There was the car, the food, and the shelter. Of course the driving. I remember that as being only my dad driving but that doesn't seem possible that one person would do all the driving. Probably my mom did some of it. But the parents aren't here to ask so I'll have to rely on my own memory.

Back to the trip. This time we were destined for Yellowstone National Park for our camping trip and planned to spend the whole vacation there, except the driving time. Yellowstone is a very large national park and there is so much to see and do there that one could easily spend weeks in that park without running out of activities or places to see. It turns out my Aunt and Uncle Schulein from California would be there along with their two kids, my cousins. These cousins were seven and ten years older than me. I'm the second oldest of four kids. The cousins really seemed more like adults than kids. The older one was a boy named John and he was about nineteen years old at the time and the girl named Mary was seventeen years old. They weren't interested in playing with us kids at that time. John went hiking and fishing with the men. Mary stuck close to her mom, my Aunt Betty. She was heard saying to her mom once, "Oh mother, she's just a child," in reference to something Rosemary said that she thought wasn't quite right. So for us kids, having cousins to meet wasn't terribly exciting. But the grown ups enjoyed being with each other as they rarely had that opportunity. One thing everyone had in common was they enjoyed the fresh air and the outdoors.

After many days of driving, we arrived at the entrance to Yellowstone National Park. How exciting. As we waited in a car lane we noticed a large pile of antlers that were confiscated from people leaving the park. Those are antlers naturally shed by animals but need to stay in the park. Also, we noticed signs that read "Do not feed the bears." This puzzled me because usually bears were behind bars in a zoo. At least the only bears I ever saw were in the zoo. So I asked about that and my mom and dad said the bears walk freely around the park here at Yellowstone. Hmm. That doesn't seem like a good idea. My brothers, sister and I fired a few rounds of questions at our parents about the safety of this. I didn't want to be at the campsite and have a bear come eat me for a snack. Our mom said the bears roam, it's really their park and we are the visitors. We must respect the bears and the rules of the park. Generally the bears are familiar with people there and they don't bother people. If we follow the park rules about bears, they will leave us alone. This is what my mom is hoping for and it's usually the way it works.

Even though there were signs saying not to feed the bears, people were doing it anyway. Some people were feeding the bears from their cars, people ahead of us. But our parents said we should keep our arms and hands inside the car and roll up the windows. Absolutely no food would go to the bears from this car. Our car is moving up closer and closer to the entrance now but mostly we are stopped, move a little forward, after a few minutes move a little more - stop and go. While we were stopped, a huge bear jumped up on it's hind legs and with a big "bam", threw his front paws directly onto the window next to our mom. She screeched, "Jim," while flying out of her seat and landing across the middle of the seat by our dad. We all screamed, loudly. The bear jumped down, bored with us. My dad said he was just looking for food. He also said that the bears only do that because so many people break the rules and feed the bears from their cars. So the bears think every car will have food for them. He stressed the importance of following the regulations the park set forth for safety. I didn't need any convincing; I would not attempt feeding the bears.

Finally we got through the gate and were assigned a camp spot. He did go to find the camp spot and make sure it was in a good place with room for the Schulein family to camp next to us. Sure enough there was room and there were two or three picnic tables and fire pits. It looked like it would work out well. We unloaded the top of the car that held the tent, tarp, cooking stove, lantern and other camping equipment.

Dad said we would walk to Old Faithful once every hour to check for the Schuleins because they didn't know where we were. Those were the days before cell phones were invented. So we took a walk to Old Faithful and watched the beautiful geyser spew its' hot water. It was an amazing site. Back in those days, you could walk as close to the geyser as you wanted. Of course you wouldn't want to get too close anyway. But you could see it well. After a while, we went back to the campsite and set up the tent, a tarp over the picnic table, a clothesline, tablecloth, cooking stove.

Prepared lanterns for the night and finally went out collecting firewood. All of this was fun. We had one very large tent for the whole family. This is where we put our suitcases, extra shoes and sleeping bags. My dad and older brother walked back to the geyser every hour until they met our cousins. Early evening, the Schulein family arrived. They began setting up camp, too.

During our first few days at Yellowstone, we did a lot of exploring. We hiked a lot and saw a variety of animals. Once we saw a very large moose. We stood behind some trees and got a very good look at the moose. His antlers were enormous. This is when my mom knew that my brother, Mike, was near sighted. He wasn't able to see the moose. And that moose was gigantic. After this vacation, Mike got glasses. Our dad, uncle, cousin, Mike and Pat made a raft of logs to go floating down the river. It was a huge project and Mike and Pat were very excited about it, practicing knot making skills. Just before the raft launch, Mike got sick with some type of bug that made him vomit and have diarrhea. He was so sorry he couldn't go on the raft but he was sick for a couple of days.

One afternoon we were at the campsite and our mom was preparing dinner. She asked me to empty the trash. I took the brown paper bag that contained the trash and walked across the narrow, dirt street to the bear proof trash receptacle. To open the trash can, I had to put down the bag of trash, slide a bar horizontally across the lid of the trash receptacle and then pull the lid up from the ground (the trash can was built into the ground) then lay it down in an open position. After that, I picked up the bag of trash and turned in the direction of the trash can, which was now an opening in the ground. As I took a step forward, I met with the face of a large, brown bear. I saw his eyes. His face was probably about 18 inches from my face, my whole body. I instantly froze; I could not move any part of my body at all. I tried to call for help but no sound would release from my throat. While frozen, I could hear hushed voices off to the side, jumbled talking. I could see in my peripheral vision, people lined up watching. It was clear they were talking to each other trying to figure out how to help. Probably someone went to get a park ranger. Still the bear and I stood facing each other, me clutching the trash bag and him waiting to eat. I didn't know why I couldn't pick my feet up or speak. But now my dad's voice tunes in. He is slowly creeping towards me with his arm fully extended; I can see this. In a low voice, he tells me to slowly move towards him. Still my body refused to move. There were voices and people moving and standing still and the only two voices I heard clearly were those of my parents. Then I heard my mom's voice clear as a bell seemingly right in my ear; never was I more glad to hear her voice. She said simply and clearly, "Put the bag down. The bear doesn't want you; he wants the trash." It was exactly the right thing to say. I don't know how she thought of it because she must have been very scared, too. But, wow, that was such a huge relief; I'd much rather that bear eat the trash than me. Now my body decided to cooperate; I immediately dropped the trash down into the hole in the ground and saw the long tongue of the bear drop straight down into the hole. My legs and arms and whole body released as I freely walked away into my parents' arms.   Now I shook and cried with relief. My mom saved my life with her words.

Grandpa Babysits

One sunny, warm afternoon, Grandpa was babysitting his three active grandsons. He attempted this feat sitting on the deck in a lawn chair under a shade umbrella with a cold glass of iced tea. He wished Grandma could have been with him to enjoy the boys and share the beautiful day, but that wasn't possible. Grandpa admired and yearned for the youth and vitality the boys possessed and couldn't resist reminiscing about his own childhood. The way they moved with grace and natural mobility - no movements of compensation for areas in the body holding onto pain. Clearly the young boys didn't possess arthritic bones or mobility issues. Grandpa was in fairly good health but his body was a bit creaky and simply didn't move as easily as it once did. The boys called out to him now and then, asking him to join in. "Come on, Grandpa, play with us." With a saddened heart, Grandpa explained why he couldn't. So they went on to play together while Grandpa watched. What could he do? It was heartbreaking but a reality he couldn't change. As Grandpa watched his active grandsons, he remembered that his grandpa told him a story when he was little, a story about making a wish and having it granted. He thought the story was made up but he pondered the notion that it was true.

The story was this: In his family, each person got one wish for a lifetime; he was granted his option for a wish when he was seven years old (the age of reason). Although allowed the wish at 7 years of age, everyone was encouraged to wait until adulthood, at least 30 years of age, before asking for this wish. Once it was used up, you couldn't get another one. Now grandpa was told stories of many family members' wishes. Some wished for money others for jobs, some for good health and others, unspoken wishes. As a boy, Grandpa was advised to be very careful in selecting his wish. So grandpa decided to wait and save his wish for a time when he really needed it. At some time in his life, he forgot all about that wish. Now, he wished so much to be able to play with his lovely grandsons, more than anything in life he had ever wished. Well, he would try it out now because he had nothing to lose and everything to gain. Grandpa wished only for what he needed - to be able to move easily, have strong muscles and bones that are pain free.

He got his wish. Grandpa's body didn't change on the outside, but inside, it felt like that of a young boy again. He looked at his skin and it looked the same. His size stayed the same. Clothes didn't magically change. But Grandpa flexed one foot, then the other. He stretched his arms overhead, they didn't hurt. Then he stood up and sat back down. Hips felt no pain. He attempted standing up, sitting on floor and standing up again. No problem; it felt as it did when he was a kid - easy and simple. Grandpa could jump, run, climb, hang from tree branches like he hasn't done in decades. He loved it. Grandpa didn't know how long this would last so he figured he better get off the deck and go play with those boys right now.

Grandpa approached the boys and said he felt better and was going to play with them; they cheered. What a treat this is. First, Grandpa played along with the games his grandsons were playing. Then he decided to teach them the games he played as a youngster; they walked to the nearby park to play these games. During the days when Grandpa was a boy, boys and girls didn't watch TV or play electronic games, they played outside with other kids. The games they played involved running, jumping, climbing, swinging, and playing with others on teams. They played stickball, kickball, various types of tag, had relay races, did acrobatic moves in the grass, and rode bicycles (Grandpa used daddy's bike). Time seemed to stand still for all of them. Finally the youngest boy noticed he was hungry. It was then they realized they were having so much fun, they played through lunch and now it was dinner time. Mommy and Daddy will wonder where everyone is.   It was time to go home now. They gathered up their toys, got on their bikes, and headed home. Daddy was driving into the garage when he saw his boys and grandpa riding bikes homes. He was shocked. Daddy turned off the car and got out right away to see if he was correct and he was. It was unbelievable that Grandpa could move about like this. The boys found it easy to believe but mommy and daddy wanted grandpa to go to a doctor and have himself checked out. They made a big deal about it and Grandpa didn't want that. The boys started talking about everything they did that day with grandpa; they were beyond excited to have this special day with grandpa.

Grandpa taught the boys what his life was like when he was a kid.   The entire day was rejuvenating for grandpa. The boys learned so much from their grandpa, more than if he only told them the stories about his childhood games. Now they have something to share with their friends about games of old.

Pat's Seeing Eye

The annual family vacation involved a lot of time in the car, on the road. Usually the vacations were about three weeks long and there were multiple destinations. Most of the time our destinations involved only our own family but sometimes we met other family members or friends at some point on our journey.

Here's the way the car configuration worked: dad drove the car, mom sat in the front in the passenger seat, a lot of stuff was in the middle of that seat and on the floor by mom's legs, three kids were in the back seat which was large enough to seat about six, and one kid sat in the far back seat which faced backwards. That very back seat could also be placed down and that kid could either sit on that or lay down and nap. The advantage of having that back seat is you could have a lot of toys and drawing materials, stuffed animals, pillows and anything at all. You had plenty of room. The disadvantage was that you might miss out on playing a game or having any conversation. The kid in the way back was the last one to know where we we headed because they were facing backwards and they were always the last one to know when we were going to stop the car and get out. In addition, if one is inclined to get car sick, it's going to happen while in that back seat. Rosemary usually sat in the back because she was the youngest kid and the smallest. At least I think that's why she sat there. She often vomited while we were driving or when we stopped. Maybe because she was backwards in the back.

While on these road trips, we traveled during the daylight hours for the most part. The only times we traveled in the dark are the first day of leaving our home and once in awhile if we were driving somewhere and had to drive a little bit after the sun went down. The first day of travel or a day when we were heading out to a new location that was a long drive, we left about three, four or five in the morning. The idea here was for the parents to get a really early start on the day while us kids were put in the car still in pajamas; parents could drive in peace for several hours while avoiding traffic. Thus they covered a lot of miles in these early morning hours. The parents stopped sometime shortly after the sun came up. We found a place to eat breakfast and change clothes, take a little break to walk around for a while and then got back on the road. The idea was to get a large portion of the drive done on the first day and by afternoon of the second day (or sometimes the third) we arrived at our first destination. As kids, it worked out fine for us; in fact it was kind of fun to leave the house in the dark in our pajamas and then end up in a place really far from home when we stopped. It must have been tiring for our parents but they probably tried a few different ways of doing it before they settled on this model.

I remember playing the alphabet game. We had to name words from signage along the way that started with the letter we had, starting in order. The person who got the z always had a more difficult time finding a word. We also played car games, calling out cars by color or brand. The guessed mileage, counted telephone poles, looked for cows grazing in fields, horses and generally anything unusual.

But my little brother, Patrick, had his very own seeing eye. The seeing eye was imaginary of course but Pat spoke of it as if it was a separate entity he carried with him and pulled out of his pocket when he felt like investigating an area. He engaged the whole car when he used his seeing eye. I recently asked my brother if he remembered the seeing eye but he doesn't recall it. We would be driving along, and Pat would usually kneel on the seat, back then we didn't use car seats or seat belts, he held his hands up to one eye and held them in a singular circle surrounding the eye. This would simulate a telescope; you get the idea. Then Pat would say in a slow and deliberate manner, "I see with my seeing eye........" The completion of the sentence was what held our interest. Sometimes it would be a mountain with snow and horses walking up or elephants walking towards a big lake; it could be an animal doing something funny or a beautiful sunset or scenery, always it was something dramatic. The seeing eye was fun. We knew it wasn't real but Pat was having so much fun with it, we loved it, too.

When Pat saw something with his seeing eye, we always looked because usually there was something he noticed along the side of the road and if not, we got a good look at the scenery. Pat did also use the seeing eye for comic relief when he became a little older. The seeing eye segments provided for conversation or started a storytelling session. It certainly added a fun dimension to our car trips.

Think about actually having a seeing eye, by seeing eye I mean that you can see whatever it is you can imagine. The seeing eye could take you to places you've never been, places you likely will never go because they are so far away and some are so very remote, beautiful places. The seeing eye could allow you to escape an uncomfortable situation, give sight to the blind, let you see people who are no longer with us but in heaven, act as a dream might act in helping you resolve problems, give you the basis for a story to tell or write, allow you to travel the world. The seeing eye could also allow you to see into different time periods. For example, a ten year old child could look into the seeing eye and find what was happening on his or her first birthday or fifth birthday, maybe even on their 50th birthday. So the seeing eye has the potential to allow something similar to time travel. One couldn't interact with the environment but just view it. The seeing eye could be used to look into the medical field in the future and learn about cures for diseases. What a wonderful thing this seeing eye can be. It could be that everyone has an opportunity to use the seeing eye if earned based on a set of criteria. What if a person could only use the seeing eye once in their life. At what age would you want to use yours? For what event would you want to use yours?

If a person could use a seeing eye once every ten years, one could see many different places and people over a lifetime. As a ten year old, your journey would be different than a twenty year of and thirty, etc. Maybe one could use the seeing eye whenever they wanted. Or there could be one seeing eye to each family and everyone shares.

Pat's seeing eye became a staple in the repertoire of games and activities to keep kids and adults distracted from having to sit still in a car for a long trip. It seemed to work really well because I still remember it sixty years after the fact. Those were good times on the vacations and in the car.

A Nature Hike in a Storm

Grandma and two grandsons prepare go on a nature hike at a nearby park. They spend a little time deciding what snacks to take and finally decide on some peanut butter sandwiches, apples, lime yogurt, and of course plenty of water. Grandma prefers to take a small blanket or tablecloth to either sit on or put on a picnic table. Grandma also threw in some ziploc bags for the boys' collections of found treasures while on the hike. For safety, Grandma packs a small first aid kit and and flashlight. The boys thought it was unnecessary to take a flashlight because it was early afternoon and the sun was shining brightly. Now that we had our necessities packed, we took some time to put on sunscreen. Nobody enjoys this process but it's something we must do to protect our skin from the sun's harmful effects. Everybody found their hats and we were ready to go. We said our goodbyes to mom, dad, and baby Fergus and loaded ourselves into the car. Sometimes we walk to Blackburn Park but today we will drive because we want to spend a lot of time hiking and don't want to be too tired to walk home afterwards.

After parking the car, we get out the backpack for grandma to carry and head to the restroom. Grandma always insists we go to the restroom before a hike and Grandma wants to go also. In another year or two, the boys will be able to carry their own backpacks on our hikes, making a lighter load for grandma.

We are ready for our hike. The path we hike is on the other side of the park. Blackburn park has two parking lots, a baseball field, gazebo, soccer field, playground, several picnic shelters, tennis courts, benches, water fountains, and lots of walking paths. We were headed to the other side of the pak to the Bird Sanctuary; that's where the entrance to the hiking trails is. We crossed a big soccer field and another green field and located the entrance to the path. The trees are so close together in this area that it's very shady and dark even on a sunny day. It's very pleasant in the heat of the summer because of this.

We entered the sanctuary and began walking on the trail. It was shady and quiet and a little cooler. We always look for treasures on the trail as we walk. Treasures of many kinds are plentiful: rocks, sticks, pine cones, interesting leaves, feathers. We pick up these treasures along the way and put them in our bags. I especially like to collect pine cones and rocks. Malachy and Rafferty both like rocks and sticks. There are often acorns which are interesting to look at.

As we looked for treasures we noticed some green leaves coming down off trees; that usually happens from wind. Of course then we noticed the tops of the trees were moving a lot, like maybe there is a storm brewing. Since we are located deep inside a very heavily wooded area, we can't tell what is happening outside the area. If a storm is brewing we won't know it unless it becomes really bad.

It was fairly dark in the sanctuary but that was fairly normal. We would check the sky next time we came to an opening in the trees. As we continued looking for our treasures, we noticed a change in temperature; it was much cooler. Now there are stronger winds and a feeling of darkness enveloping us.

The sky turns dark. Thunder crashes loudly and lightening like white daggers in the sky. The rains come. The ground is so slick on the path, they may not be able to make it out in time.

We talked about going back and getting to the open field and then heading to the shelter. But is an open field the place to be in the middle of a storm? No, we searched for shelter and as we spied an area that could keep us safe from the storm, we saw the storm clouds pass by and the sun surface. We all agreed to finish our nature hike and then go home to eat our snacks and change into dry clothes. Next time we will bring rain ponchos.

Guardian Angels

A young mom was recently divorced and moved to a new city with her two young children. As this was a difficult time for her, she felt she might need family support as she navigated this new single parenting journey. So she moved to the city where she was raised, to be closer to her family, This mom found a place to live, a nice house that was just a few blocks away from her loving Aunt Rose and Uncle Larry. They helped her as the family became accustomed to the new surroundings. It was July when they made the move and Mo had plenty of time to register the kids for school, which she did. Colleen will be in second grade and Ryan in first grade. They didn't have any friends yet in this new place but that would soon change. One Sunday, Aunt Rose and Uncle Larry picked us up for church. Together, they went to Mass and afterwards Uncle Larry said we would sign up the kids for soccer. Mo didn't know anything about soccer and neither did the kids. She told Uncle Larry this and he said, "You will, soon." He and Aunt Rose said this would be a good way for us to make some new friends. And soccer practice will start before school starts so the kids will meet other kids who will be in the same classroom as them. That seemed like a really good idea to me so we signed them up and got all the necessary information about practice, uniforms, times, and locations. Colleen and Ryan seemed happy and excited about this. That was a really good start to their first week in this new city.

The next day, Monday, Aunt Rose and Uncle Larry came to Mo's house and said, "Now we want to show you the Recreation Center." This sounded like a great idea so we got everyone together and loaded ourselves up in the car. they drove to the Rec Center and when they approached the parking lot, Mo was surprised at how large it was. Inside the family took a quick tour; the Rec Center had many rooms for meetings and parties, a large gym with basketball courts and bleachers, racquetball courts, an indoor pool, outdoor pool with small toddler area and big slide, diving boards both high and low. Outside that area were a large complex of baseball fields, a large lake, hiking trails and picnic areas. This was a beautiful community center where people came together to relax, play, exercise. Mo was very excited to learn that we would have access to this center simply by being a resident of the neighborhood. The price for this was very low and they joined. So they could go to the rec center as often as they wanted, year round.

At this time, the family had about six weeks before school started so they went to the pool almost daily. While there, Colleen and Ryan played in the water and Mo lounged and read books poolside. It was most delightful and really took the edge off this transitional period in our lives. Colleen and Ryan met some kids from the neighborhood at the pool and Mo met some moms. Spending time at the rec center during that time made the transition feel more like a vacation than a big change. It was just what everyone needed.

Aunt Rose and Uncle Larry were special angels for that family. Mo believes in angels, guardian angels and thinks sometimes they come to us in the form of people.

These people definitely fit that bill. And that never changed, even years later. They always seemed to be there for the family at just the right time with the knowledge to do just what was needed. At this time, Mo's parents didn't live in St. Louis, but they did move back later when the dad retired. There is no one like one's parents but Aunt Rose and Uncle Larry were filling in for now and what an amazing job they did.

One day in the spring, Colleen had her First Communion. It was a big and exciting event, one in which all prepared for, for months - all school year. There was preparation at school for Colleen. At home, Mo shopped for new outfits, cleaned the house, prepared food for a party; it was busy and exciting. People came into St. Louis from out of town. Grandma and Grandpa McGovern came from Illinois and they stayed with us. Colleen and Ryan's dad, Grandma Murphy, Aunt Mary, Uncle Sonny and cousins came from Kansas City. They stayed somewhere else as there were too many to stay with us.

The Church service and First Communion was beautiful; the family took pictures with the priest and classmates. Afterwards, the party started. Everyone went to Mo's house and people arrived for food, conversation and fun. Fortunately the weather was beautiful with warm temperatures and sunny skies. This was especially nice because they had a big yard with plenty of space for kids to play and run around; there was also plenty of space for grown ups to sit and relax and eat and drink. The cousins didn't get to see each other very often so they played with the soccer ball and kept busy with all sorts of games. The kids knew when it was time for the parents to go, and were not on board with that. There would even be some resistance and begging. But that goes with the territory and the grownups were ready for it.

What Mo didn't expect was how let down she would feel when everyone left. Aside from a few friends and the Mackens, when everyone else left, they left town. That left kind of sad and Mo definitely felt a wave of loneliness sweep over her rather intensely as she cleaned up. Colleen and Ryan were ok; they were having fun playing with each other so they didn't seem to notice how their mom was feeling. But cleaning up kept mom busy and distracted as much as possible. Mo put away all the excess food and extra chairs. Finally she was finished with these tasks and was ready to sit down and relax; again she felt very sad. Mo really missed her parents a lot and her siblings; and she missed the kids having their cousins to play with. But just then, the phone rang. It was an unexpected call from the Mackens; unexpected because they had been Mo's house for much of the day. But they thought the family would like to go to Dairy Queen for some ice cream and then stop by the park to play for a bit. Certainly the family didn't need any ice cream because they had tons of leftover food at home, including remnants of a celebratory First Communion cake.   The family, at least Mo, did need the company. So off they went to Dairy Queen and took ice cream down the street to the park. They sat at a picnic table and ate ice cream and talked about the fun party. It was relaxing and comforting for Mo. Then Colleen and Ryan went to the playground and played for a while. By the time they went home, Mo didn't feel that sense of loneliness, but instead felt loved by these beautiful angels who were her aunt and uncle. How blessed were they all. Years later, about thirty, Mo told Aunt Rose how she felt that day and how comforting it was for them to come to the family at just the right time. I often wondered if they sensed how Mol felt or simply anticipated it might be hard, especially since Mo was now doing this all on her own. Aunt Rose said she didn't really remember it too well. Mol remembers it because it was such high impact. Mo cherishes those memories and guardian angels. Mo knows Uncle Larry is looking out for us all from heaven, along with Mo's parents and Aunt Rose is doing the same here on earth. She is ninety three years old now and still praying for us all and helping people whenever and wherever she can.

The guardian angels helped make the family's transition to this new environment and this new family configuration as smooth as possible. They made everyone feel as safe and secure as possible. In addition to all they were a lot of fun to be around.

The very first year the family lived in Bissell Hills, Aunt Rose and Uncle Larry took the kids every morning and fed them breakfast then took them to school. This was to help Mo out as she had to go to work earlier than the kids had to go to school. As a retired person Mo realizes what a huge sacrifice that must have been for them to get up and moving and be responsible for these two children every day early. Aunt Rose and Uncle Larry went to Mass daily so they said it was no problem to take Colleen and Ryan with them. Of course they didn't have to do the breakfast thing but they happily did. Colleen and Ryan still remember pancakes shaped in their initials. Aunt Rose always made things fun for them.

When the kids were too sick to go to school, the Mackens took them in for a day or two. They could nap on the couch where Aunt Rose could keep an eye on them. She would take their temperatures when necessary, feed them soup or whatever they wanted or needed at the time. Most importantly, she made them feel loved.

Life is a series of transitions. Sometimes people don't want it to be; they want things to freeze or slow down at certain times to savor the joy and wonder of it all. Now Mo is in the same transitional stage the Mackens were in when they cared for my kids, maybe even be slightly older. Mo only hopes her continued life transitions can be as graceful as those guardian angels, Rosemary and Larry.

Field of Ivy

The Murphy house was situated on a busy street so usually when the boys played outside, they went to the back yard. Their backyard was pretty but not very large. Also the back yard had a very uneven slant in a couple places. Often the boys went to Blackburn Park to play where there was plenty of room. Today they decided to play in the back field, adjacent to the back yard.

Outside the sliding glass door from the kitchen to the deck is a view of the back yard. With the position of the house to the surrounding streets, one can look one hundred and eighty degrees and see back yards and many very large trees. It's all green. The trees are old and plentiful; birds and owls enjoy their homes in these beautiful trees. As one looks out, she notices the depth of back neighboring yards is vast; there is a lot of land. You can still see most of the houses but there is enough land to make it appear much like a park. The front of the house was noisy but the back of the house was very quiet, mostly due to the large, old trees and wide open fields.

Mr. and Mrs. Goodheart own a vast part of the property in back of the Murphy's fence. They are an older couple whose children are grown up and moved away. The Goodhearts said the Murphy boys can play in their fields any time they want. This is good news for Malachy and Rafferty. They went out back to play on a lovely Fall evening just before dinner. It was still daylight but because the dark came sooner now, they wouldn't have a great deal of time to play back there. But that seemed like it would work out well because their dinner would be ready soon anyway.

The field behind the Murphy's fence is where the boys were headed. The field was lined with bushes and some short fencing but had many trees throughout and was completely covered with ivy. There was no grass. This was not poison ivy, but another type of non poisonous ivy. The ivy had been growing wild for years and was never cut or trimmed. Often the ivy was deep in certain areas and shallow in others. It was a deep green color, indicating a very healthy and strong ivy. By looking at the ivy on the ground, it was impossible to tell how deep it was. Also, it was impossible to know what was underneath the ivy. When walking through the ivy, one needs to take high steps and carefully navigate the area. While walking, if ivy wraps around even a small part of your shoe, you will trip. Certainly you must walk so that the ivy doesn't grab your leg.

One day the whole family went to the field, not to play but just to walk. Baby Fergus thought it was fun but he couldn't negotiate the ivy and uneven surfaces at all. Grandma Mo had to be very slow about walking back to the house, too. While walking in the back fields is challenging for most, certainly for me, the boys love it. They find the uneven and invisible ground to be fun, like a game. If watching them from the deck, you will often see them walking or running and then down on the ground because it's impossible to see the potholes through the ivy. But they don't mind; in fact that's exactly what they like. It' somewhat unpredictable and different every time they go out. This is very unlike playing indoors on an even and flat surface, although there's a time and place for that also.

On this fall afternoon, as the boys were exploring, they usually stick pretty close to each other but sometimes one will run faster or see something to explore that must be investigated immediately. They other one then catches up, mostly out of curiosity but also from a sense of brotherly love. One can't help but to notice both boys look after each other whether they are home or away.

Then it was quiet for a few seconds and Malachy noticed Rafferty was nowhere to be seen. He called out for his brother as he looked around in every direction. But all he saw was ive. Malachy looked upwards towards the trees, thinking Rafferty may have climbed up a tree. No Rafferty. Malachy ran, walked, tripped, all the while yelling, "Rafferty, Rafferty, answer me Rafferty." No response.

Meanwhile, Rafferty slipped through the ivy and into a hole where he couldn't be seen from the top of the ivy. Now Rafferty sinks down, down, and down. He is scared and yelling, "help." But nobody hears him. It's very dark on his way down through the thick ivy and earth. Finally he reaches the bottom. Rafferty can not see anything in the dark and has to feel around to realize he is in a tunnel. It's a little cold down there and he didn't dress for that. He has no flashlight so he can't see what's in front of him. Now he is very afraid and is calling out, "Malachy. Where are you? Malachy, help." This went on for a while and he starts to cry, not knowing what to do. Just then he heard a noise; it was probably a field mouse and Rafferty isn't afraid of them. In fact if it is a field mouse, Rafferty will attempt to follow him out to daylight and safety.

Malachy is beside himself searching for Rafferty. At one point, he went in the house, thinking maybe Rafferty just went inside to rest or had to go to the bathroom. His mom asked what he was doing. When Malachy realized Rafferty wasn't inside, he said, "Oh, I just have to go to the bathroom." Mom said, "What is Rafferty doing out there?" Malachy said that Rafferty is exploring. That is true even though Malachy doesn't know where Rafferty is exploring. He doesn't want to tell mom until he has explored every option and given up on finding Rafferty. Malachy believes he will find his brother. So he grabs a flashlight without mom seeing and heads back to the field. This time he retraced his steps and his brothers steps. Sometimes the holes that lead to the tunnels can be only one step apart from each other. You can be standing right next to each other and one of you will fall into the hole and the other won't. Once you know about the holes, you can avoid them if you want. But Malachy didn't yet know about the holes in the ground that are covered with layers of dark green ivy.

Rafferty listens for that mouse again and hears it scampering. It's going fast through the tunnel and has not vision problems. Rafferty can't keep up with the mouse but definitely can hear the direction in which he is traveling He calls out, "Hello, hello, is anybody here? Malachy, can you hear me? I hope you can find me." Raff can hear his own voice bouncing against the earthen walls. Now he hears people talking in the distance. Raff searches and searches for the people whose voices he hears. Suddenly he sees dim light as he walks through the tunnel. Then the voices get louder. He finds a big room behind a rod iron gate. Children are in there playing as if nothing weird is going on and the lights are on in their ceiling. Raff stopped and asked them what was going on and where he was. The kids were in their own basement; they knew there was a tunnel but never went inside the tunnel. It turns out those kids were the McMichael kids. They live in one of the houses that back up into the fields behind the Murphy house. Raff is in preschool with Raelin and was surprised to see her so close. Raff asked them to let him in because he was scared in the dark tunnel. The opened the gate. Raff was so relieved but he said, "Wait, I have to go back outside and find my brother, Malachy." They said that he didn't have to go back through the tunnel but could just go outside their back door. So he did and Raelin and her brother Wyatt went with Raff.

They all went outside to help Raff find Malachy but Rafferty heard his mom calling him in for dinner. He was happy to hear about dinner because he was starving; it had been many hours since he last ate. But Rafferty looked around and noticed Malachy was nowhere to be seen. Knowing his brother well, he knew Malachy would be out looking for him. So the three kids each climbed their own tree, hoping to get a good view of the area and locate Malachy quickly. No Malachy to be found anywhere. So Raffety found the hole in the ivy, showed it to Raelin and Wyatt and down they all went. This time Raff knew where he was going. Raelin left the basement lights on so soon enough they would wind up at home. They all walked through the tunnel and found that it had several places where it shot out in different directions; it may not be as simple to find their basement as they thought. So they all stuck together and called Malachy's name repeatedly. At some point he would turn up. And so down the long tunnel, they saw a light flashing from the floor to the ceiling and from side to side. Guess who it was? Malachy. And just in time for dinner. Rafferty said they really had to hurry if they were to get home and in the house in time for dinner without having to tell mom and dad where they had been. Raff said, "Come on, I'll tell you about it as we run back home. We're going through the basement at Raelin's house." So they went back home and had dinner with mom and dad. Rafferty always carried a flashlight after that.

Mom asked if they had fun playing outside and they said yes. Dad asked if they found anything fun or interesting while they explored and they both looked at each other and then back and dad and said, … "Oh, just the usual."

The Night Flyer

Once upon a time there was a little boy named Gus and a mom named Margo. Gus was four years old and didn't have any brothers or sisters. He had a dad named Pete and a cat named Tilda. Gus went to preschool three morning per week and spent the rest of his time with his mom, Margo. They went everywhere together and did everything together.

Sometimes when mom picked up Gus from preschool, they went to a nearby park and had their lunch that mom had packed. After lunch, Gus played on the playground or they went on a short walk on one of the trails. Gus enjoyed this special time at the park with mom. On some of these days, other kids were also playing at the park and Gus had fun playing with them.

During cold or rainy weather, mom and Gus usually went home. Gus was free to play with his toys or play imaginary games while mom made lunch for them. He always enjoyed this time at home also and mom usually made something for lunch that he liked.

Then there were other days when mom picked up Gus from pre school and then they ran errands. He didn't so much enjoy these days because it involved going to some dull places and then he got very hungry during the whole trip. But mom would take him out to lunch after the errands and make sure he got something he really liked for lunch, maybe even a treat.

In all of these scenarios, one thing was constant. After lunch, mom and Gus always went upstairs to his bedroom, sat in a comfortable chair with mom while she read him a story. Gus had so many books, mom's childhood books, dad's childhood books and Gus's very own books. Sometimes mom told a story but Gus had so many books, they read a story most of the time. After the story, Gus took a nap and mom went downstairs and did whatever it is that mom's do when their kids are napping.

One day, mom was reading a book to Gus. This book had a lovely picture of the Eiffel Tower which mom pointed out to Gus. He said, "Yeah, that looks pretty much like the real one." Mom thought that was Gus's way of being funny. Gus did enjoy a joke or a prank so this didn't seem unusual. But mom began to see a trend here. With a number of books, as Gus saw the pictures, he said things that indicated he had seen that place in person. Of course we are talking about places he had never been such as lions in Africa, icebergs in Antarctica, the Sistine Chapel, The Arch, so many places.

Mom thought maybe this way of joking had gone far enough. She talked with Dad about it and they decided to talk with Gus's teachers at preschool to see if this is happening at school. They did speak with his teachers and the teachers confirmed that when they are learning about a new place, Gus often does say he has been there. It has happened so many times that the teachers thought Gus and his family very likely could not have traveled that much. They, in fact, were about to request a meeting with the parents to discuss this. They want to reach some solution on how to deal with it. On the surface, it looks like Gus is making up stories, lying. This is what mom and dad thought also. Mom and dad will talk with Gus about this the next time it comes up. They decided to ask Gus for explanations when he says he already knows about a place that they know they haven't taken him to.

The very next day, as mom and Gus are picking a book to read, Gus asked for a book with the Pyramids of Egypt. Mom couldn't find that specific of a book on the pyramids but she did find one with generic pictures of pyramids. So mom began reading the book and Gus was happy with the story. But when they reached the page with a picture of a pyramid, Gus said that wasn't the right one. He said that is not one of the Pyramids of Egypt. Mom asked him why he said that and Gus responded, "Because I've been there and that doesn't look the same." With this statement, mom thinks now that Gus is having trouble distinguishing between reality and fantasy. But she decides to go along with him for now and dig a little deeper into what's going on with him. So mom says, "I don't know exactly how you know that but this is a nice picture of a pyramid so we'll pretend for the sake of this story." Gus says that's ok with him.

The next day for story time, mom read a book about a mountain climber. The climber succeeded in climbing Mount Everest. Here we go again. Gus said, "Oh yeah, that is so pretty and you can see so far when standing at the top." Mom asked Gus how he knows this and he said, "Because I've been there and seen it." This time mom asked more questions, when were you there and how did you get there? Daddy and I didn't take you. Gus laughed and said, "Of course I know you and dad didn't take me." Mom said again, "How did you get there?" Gus said, "Well, I travel at night, after dark." "I'm a night flyer." Mom asked what that meant. What in the world is a night flyer? Gus said being a night flyer is only for kids. He has seen other kid night flyers and they're all under ten years old. What happens is during that time when you are falling asleep, just before you fall asleep, you are somehow lifted up and outside of your house. Then your body takes flight. It's nice because even in the cold or rain, you stay the same comfortable temperature you were when you were in bed falling asleep. You don't know where you will go; it could be someplace close to home or very far away. Usually the place you fly to is a place you talked about in school or home or read a story about or thought about but it could be anywhere.

Mom was shocked by this explanation and didn't know what to think about it. She felt she needed to ask Gus questions about the process to try to understand. Mom thought she would hold off until she speaks with dad and possibly gets advice from a professional as to how to proceed. Mom and dad are strongly rooted in reality and find this situation extremely puzzling. They felt like it couldn't be true; of course people don't fly, kids don't fly. Mom, dad and Gus will all have a chat about being a night flyer.

After dinner that night night, mom, dad, and Gus all stayed at the table for a talk. Dad said, "Gus, mom and I want to talk with you about your night flying. Mom told me what you said about it and I'd like to hear about it from you.

Gus said, "Sure. Here's what happens. When I'm just about asleep at night, I somehow end up outside just above the house. Then I take flight and end up in a destination that I didn't pick. The destination is a place that I might have been thinking about or heard about in school or at home, sometimes during a story." "I've been to a lot of places. There are other night flyers, kids no older than ten years old. I've not interacted with any of them but I've seen them. I don't fly every night and don't know when it will happen."

Dad asked, "Is it ever scary? "

Gus replied, "No, it's never scary. It's exciting and I always feel safe when flying."

Mom said, "Have you told anyone about this?"

Gus said, "I have, but I think people don't believe me so I just don't talk about it anymore."

More question formulated, like can you take other people with you? How many nights a week do you fly? Do you feel tired or different in any way after you fly? How long do you think you are gone on a flight usually? Can you take anything with you when you fly? Like a camera?

Mom, dad and Gus did their usual bedtime routine, tucking in Gus. Mom and dad decided that it seemed Gus was safe and he wasn't troubled in any way be this. In fact the one part that could be hard for him is when he tells people and they don't believe him. He doesn't feel compelled to make them believe him but feels good about being honest and they don't make fun of him because they think he's joking.

Mom and dad talked about it after Gus went to bed and decided not to worry but instead think of how it could work for Gus. Gus has a unique opportunity to learn about the world. He can visit anyplace at all. Some places he visits will be in different time zones so while it's night time for Gus, it's daytime for them. In fact, mom and dad can even to some degree influence where Gus goes by talking about places and putting a bug in his ear. How fun will it be to learn about all the places Gus goes. Up until now, he hasn't talked with his parents about it, only pointing out places as they read stories. It's going to be really nice to be able to talk with Gus about his night flying. In fact, they just may make that a part of his regular bedtime routine, to tell about where he has been. Maybe Gus can even help with planning family vacations.

After tucking Gus into bed that night, mom and dad sat on the couch to relax. Mom said to dad, "Where do you think our son will go tonight?"

A Bit of Family History for the Boys

As an adult, I have thought many times that I so wish I might have listened to stories of my parents and grandparents when I was growing up. At the time it seemed they were always talking about people I didn't know but they thought I knew. It also seemed like they were telling the same stories over and over again. That may have been true. But there might be a very good reason to tell a story over and over again. Back then, I tuned much of it out. By the time I developed a strong interest in my family history, my parents and grandparents were gone.

In two thousand eleven, I took a trip to Ireland with two of my siblings and six of my cousins. We toured many places, but ultimately the most fascinating was the birth home of our paternal grandfather. In doing this we met several of our second cousins. Before this trip, I studied the family tree and learned as much as I could. But the cousin who took us to the grandfather's home, which is still in the family, told us stories about staying there when she was a little girl. The experience was unforgettable. Those cousins were on my dad's side of the family.

On my mom's side of the family, I still have an aunt who will answer questions regarding family history; she's ninety three and has an excellent memory. She is one who enjoyed the details in life so that helps with the storytelling even today.

On a Friday evening in mid summer, two little boys packed their backpacks and went to their Grandmother's house for an overnight visit. They packed their toothbrushes, toothpaste, pajamas, clothes for the next day, stuffed animals to sleep with and a few other little things like legos and pokemans.

Oftentimes, Grandma Mo has a special activity planned for the boys either on the evening they stay over or on the next morning. Sometimes we go out to an organized event. But this time nothing was planned. It was a very hot summer day and everyone was quite happy to stay home and inside for the whole visit. It turned out to be a most delightful visit, this visit of doing nothing. Because we did a lot of talking.

First, when the boys arrived, they told Grandma about everything they brought with them, not because Grandma needed to know as much as they were so excited to share. This warms Grandma's heart because she knows they are soon to grow up and mayl not be of such open hearts. Grandma knows to savor this sweet time. They don't know it yet, but this time will fly. Next, they take their bags upstairs to their room where they share a big, soft bed together. They get their toothbrushes and paste and put them in the bathroom and put their slippers next to the bed along. They put their stuffed animals in the bed in preparation for bedtime and then they take a bit of time to roll around on the bed. They open the shutters and look out into the street and into the neighbor's windows. It's like taking inventory. They like the change of venue.

Now it's time to go back downstairs to do whatever it is we will do. Here are some possible activities: playing with tiny legos, lincoln logs, animals, playdough, puzzles drawing, playing with musical instruments, knitting, making forts, and reading. There is also the occasional tv show or movie. Grandma tries to limit that as much as possible because it's best to have them engaged and active. But there are those times. Their favorite activities are cyclical. For a while they are into the animal play, sometimes it's the fort building, or the lincoln logs. Grandma likes to keep a variety of toys at home, especially ones that are different than they have at their house. They also have recently learned to play candyland and go fish. These are games they usually wouldn't play at home because there's more running about and possibly some fighting. But that doesn't happen at Grandma Mo's house. The boys act like angels. That works out well for everyone. This seems like the most fun part of the visit but that is yet to come.

Next it's dinner time. Everybody goes into the kitchen and the boys sit at the table while Grandmas prepares dinner. If dinner will take a bit of time to prepare, the boys will have drawing paper and crayons and create pictures while waiting. Then dinner and the boys want to hop upstairs to bed. They don't ever try to talk Grandma into staying up too late because they don't want to miss out on the storytime feature of the bedtime routine. That is the most fun part of the visit for all three of them.

To go upstairs in Grandma's house is fun because the stairs are slightly hidden by a door. So going upstairs has an air of quiet and intimacy that somehow downstairs bedrooms don't have. The only rooms upstairs are bedrooms and a bathroom. So up they go with glee. Sometimes they sing or hum because they're so happy. First thing they do is take off their clothes, then they brush their teeth and put their pajamas on. There might be some chit chat and running about, throwing their stuffed animals up in the air, tumbling on the floor - the usual things kids do before bed. Grandma Mo always reminds the boys about two things before they go to bed. The first thing is to stay away from the steps if they get up in the night; there's a little gate as a reminder. The second thing is they can always come in Grandma's room in the night if they anything at all, even if Grandma's asleep. And she will be asleep. It' rare there's any issue during the night but it has happened a few times. If the boys get up to go to the bathroom, they are able to see well because there are nightlights in every room. Safety and comfort are Grandma's two top priorities.

Here's the fun part of the whole visit - story time. The boys typically request a scary story from Grandma. Grandma obliges but always resolves the scary story with a nice, safe ending. Grandma doesn't want boys really scared before going to sleep. This night, one boy noticed the framed picture on the dresser. He said, "Can I see that and hold it?" Grandma handed the framed picture to the grandson. He named the people in the picture, "Grandma Alice and Grandpa James." Grandma said, "Yes, that's right. Would you like me to tell you about them?" Both little guys said, "Yes." Grandma told them she would tell them about their great grandparents but that would be their story for the night because it will take a little while. They said that was ok because they want to hear about their great grandparents.

This is very special now because the boys are lying in bed, the house is quiet and one of them is probably going to fall asleep during the story. The first thing Grandma told them is Grandma Alice and Grandpa James' parents came to this country from Ireland. So, as children Alice and James did not know their grandparents - they never had a chance to meet. Alice and James were born in the years nineteen twenty and nineteen twenty one.

Your Grandma Alice, named Alice Margaret Macken, had two brothers, both older; their names were Larry and Russell. Alice's Dad was a streetcar driver. You can see an original streetcar in University City; we can go there sometime. Alice's mom worked as a maid in the homes of very well to do folks; in some jobs, she lived in the house with other maids. Sometime I can show you one of those houses in the Central West End; it's quite large. After she was married, she stayed home to care for the children, house and her husband. She also cared for two nieces, Catherine and Marie. One of her sisters who immigrated to the United States had two girls but she lost her husband and had to work long hours so Alice's mom (also Alice) took them in. At times this may have been hard on Alice because her mom was so occupied with many other family members. Alice had a surgery on her collarbone when she was about ten years old. She couldn't write with her right hand and had to learn to write with her left hand. As a result she developed extremely poor penmanship. When Alice was about eleven years old, her older brother, Russell, died. He became ill and couldn't return to good health. This was very sad for Alice and her whole family, especially her mom. Around this time, Alice met the McGovern family who lived close by. Kay was Alice's age and James was close in age. At eleven years of age, they didn't expect that they would later marry. But they did. That's part of the way you boys got here. Then when Alice was in high school, her mom became very ill. It was a number of years before the doctors found out what was wrong and then they were able to fix it. During high school, one of Alice's friends was Kay McGovern. Kay had a brother named James. Yes, that's your Grandpa James. He and Alice were married at a later date. After high school, Alice went to work for an outfit called the Queen's Work. At this job, Alice worked with a very good friend, Jane Sudhoff. She also met and became friends with Rosemary Hendron. Later, Alice introduced Rosemary to her brother Larry. Rosemary and Larry dated and later married. This is Great Great Aunt Rosemary Macken who you know. Her husband, Larry, is deceased; you never had the chance to meet him. We call her Aunt Rose and she is now ninety three years old.

Still awake?

Let's catch up with Grandpa James. He has a mom, Mary Anne Gilvarry and dad, Dennis Ambrose McGovern, both from Ireland. These are your great great grandparents who were deceased long before you were born. Because they immigrated from Ireland, James never met his grandparents because they were too far away and back in those days people did not travel as much as today. James had an older sister, Betty, who is still alive and living in California; he had another sister named Kay, and brother named Dan. Dan is the dad of the cousins house we go to every year on the day after thanksgiving. James' mom stayed home and cared for the house and family. We don't know what she did prior to getting married. James' dad was a railroad worker. As a child, James had some jobs that we might consider unusual today. One job was preparing the fires for Jewish people in their homes on Jewish holidays; he got paid for this. Also in the nineteen thirties he sold vegetables from his Uncle Mike's vegetable truck and sometimes he even drove that truck, even though he was only fourteen years old. When James was older, in high school, did dad lost his leg in an accident at work. This was a very challenging situation for Dennis to cope with. The recovery was difficult and painful. Back in those days, the prosthetics were made of wood, which was heavy and uncomfortable. Today there are different materials that make it easier for people who need them. There were some times that followed that were financially hard for Dennis and his family. They were forced to move to a different place on two occasions. In fact, they would have been among the homeless if it weren't for friends who helped them out. A family called the Flynns had an apartment they rented to Dennis and family, likely with low rent. Betty married Vernon and moved to a small town in Missouri for a while during Vernon's school or internship. James went into the military, the Army. He served in World War II and spent time in France and Germany. James was shot in the leg and had shrapnel in his leg, around the shin, his whole life. He said he didn't feel it but it showed up on cat scans. After the war, James returned home and went to Rolla School of Mines to become an engineer, which he did.

This is the place where Alice and James get together. The last year he was in school, Alice was with him. They married on June fourteenth, nineteen forty seven. Then they packed up and went to Rolla for James' last year of school. They seemed to enjoy this year of school. At the end of the school year, James was offered a job in St. Louis as a mechanical engineer for Shell Oil Company. He took that job and they moved to St. Louis and into an apartment next to some of their friends, the Sudhoffs and the Mackens. They had about a year to two years there and their first child was born while they lived their, Michael Russell McGovern, you know him as Great Uncle Mike; he is married to Janine. Baby Mike was with Alice and James in the apartment and Alice and James started planning on buying a house. During this time, Alice became pregnant with Maureen, you know her as Grandma Mo. Alice and James and Mike moved into their new house in June of nineteen fifty one, a month before Maureen was born. Now there were four. That house was in Glasgow Village in North County. Some day Grandma Mo will take you for a drive and point out the house to you. Two more children were born there, Patrick in nineteen fifty three and Rosemary in nineteen fifty five. Patrick is your Great Uncle Pat and he is with Aunt Shu, Rosemary is Great Aunt

Rosemary Hollis and she is married to Great Uncle Tom. They live in California. Rosemary and Tom have three daughters, Audrey, Laura and Emma; they are your dad's first cousins and your first cousins once removed.

Alice, James and their four kids, Mike, Maureen, Pat and Rosemary, all lived in the house on Estridge for twelve years. Then they moved to a brand new house on a street called Wheatfield in Florissant, Missouri. This was a bigger house with a smaller yard; it had two bathrooms instead of one and four bedrooms instead of three. There was a nice patio with a privacy fence in the back and enough room in the yard to play softball or soccer. The house had a nice basement. The whole neighborhood was brand new and there were plenty of kids to play with and go to school with. Grandpa James was still working at Shell Oil and Grandma Alice was taking care of the house and family. For a few years Alice got a job working for a company doing payroll. She liked that job a lot. They lived in that house until nineteen seventy one. At that time, James was transferred to California for his job. He had to go or lose his job so he decided to go. Maureen went to college in Missouri so was only in California for summers and Christmas. Pat and Rose were in high school in California and Mike was working probably. Alice was thrilled with the ability to grow lots of flowers in her yard all year long. In California, the seasons did change but temperature didn't vary a lot so it allowed for avocado trees, figs, lots of roses and other flowers. Alice learned a lot about the climate relating to growing flowers and plants. Patrick and Rosemary graduated from college. Maureen got married in nineteen seventy two in St. Louis Missouri. She married Pat Murphy who you know as Grandpa Murphy. He lives in Kansas City Missouri. He sends you birthday and Christmas presents.

Around the year nineteen seventy eight, Grandpa James was transferred for his job once more. This time he was transferred to Bloomington, Illinois. He accepted that job and he and Grandma Alice moved there. Rosemary stayed in California going to school. It is unclear what Mike and Pat were doing during that time. Alice and James moved into an even bigger house in Bloomington with a big yard. They had a dog named George who enjoyed going for walks and playing in the yard. The neighbors got to know George and loved him. Alice and James made new friends in Bloomington, friends from James' work, the neighborhood and church. They often traveled to St. Louis to visit family. At that time Grandma Mo lived in St. Louis with children Colleen and Ryan, that's your Aunt Colleen and daddy. They also lived close to Great Aunt Rosemary and Great Uncle Larry Macken. When Alice and James visited they stayed with Maureen and spent time with Colleen and Ryan, too, also Rosemary and Larry. Sometimes Maureen packed with the car and took Colleen and Ryan for a weekend visit to see Alice and James in Bloomington, Illinois.

Alice and James stayed in that house for seven or eight years. Then James retired from his job. That house was too big for them and even though they had really good friends there, they wanted to be around family. Most of their family was in St. Louis, Missouri. So that is where they moved.

So the year was nineteen eighty four. Your daddy was nine years old and Aunt Colleen was ten. Maureen, Grandma Mo, was thirty three years old. Back then Grandma has darker hair and could move easier. They were all very excited when Alice and James moved to St Louis. They had a house with an extremely large yard. James built a lovely rose garden for Alice. The house had three bedrooms and two bathrooms upstairs. The basement had a large work area, a large play area with a ping pong table, and a room that could be used as a bedroom but was used as an office. Also there was a bathroom and a bar with a sink and refrigerator. James installed all of those things in the basement. His brother, Dad, helped with electricity. It was a great place to have a party. It was about the same space as the basement in your house. Just arranged and decorated a little differently.

A fun part of the house was that when family members visited, they had plenty of room to stay at Alice and James' house. That may have been in their thoughts when deciding what house to buy. Alice and James liked that the house was only a couple miles away from the Mackens and Maureen, Colleen and Ryan. They also liked being very close to their church; they sometimes walked there. Their house was very comfortable except for one thing. They both smoked cigarettes in the house and it made for a bad smell. They started smoking many years earlier when the health risks of smoking were not well known. By the time they knew of the harm smoking can cause, they were so involved with it, they couldn't stop. It's hard to explain how that works but always say no to anything in your body involving smoke and you won't have to be concerned about it.

In nineteen eighty seven, Alice and James' kids arranged a party for them, at their house. It was a great idea, a nice way to celebrate their fortieth anniversary. While all arranged and ready to do, on the morning of the party, Larry Macken died. Everyone knew that he was getting ready to die but didn't know (can never know) exactly when. Alice and James were told about the surprise party and asked the kids to cancel it. That is what happened. After a lot of phone calls, the party was off. Everyone was sad about Larry dieing and will miss him greatly. It was time to prepare goodbyes. Remember Larry is Alice's brother.

It was shortly after this time that Mike McGovern, your Great Uncle Mike, moved back to St. Louis from Indiana. He stayed at Alice and James' house with his very large dog named Friday. Friday was kind of old, very large and as friendly as a dog could be. She slept a lot. She even let people dress her up in people's clothes. Rosemary (Hollis) dressed her in a hat, glasses, pearl necklace and a lovely flowered dress. Friday was agreeable. Alice and James loved Friday very much. Mike was looking for jobs and finally he found a good job. This was in nineteen ninety one. The job Mike got was at AT&T. Guess who he met there? Janine, Great Aunt Janine. One day Alice said to

James and Maureen, "Something is going on with Mike. I think he must have a date." We asked why she thought that. Alice said, "Well, Mike is outside cleaning his truck. He never cleans the truck. That's what makes me think he has a date." It turns out she was right. Mike was preparing his car to go on his first date with Janine. Mike and Janine met at a training session at work and one day Janine gave Mike her phone number and asked that he call her. Mike took that as a clue she might want to go on a date with him. He was right. They settled on a date to go out and Mike scrubbed up his truck. He wanted to present a good image. That has been about twenty five years ago now. Alice was more excited than anyone because she wanted Mike to have a lady in his life. For Alice's birthday in October, Mike brought Janine to a family dinner to celebrate, at Maureen's house. The family started to get to know Janine through this event and others following. In nineteen ninety five, Mike and Janine got married. Alice and James had a really nice party in their basement to get Janine's family and Mike's family together to have dinner and celebrate the upcoming wedding. They married in April of nineteen ninety five.

Now Alice and James were alone in the house. They traveled to Ireland to visit some relatives. In nineteen ninety six they traveled to Spain with their good friends, the Hennekees.

Alice had one more year of life before she died, but she didn't know it yet. In the summer of nineteen ninety six, Maureen (Grandma Mo) was off work and able to spend a lot more time with Alice than usual. They did a lot of shopping together and going out to lunch. It was a lot of fun. When the next year rolled around, Alice wasn't feeling too well. About January or February she learned she was sick and by March, she was gone. Ryan came home from college to say goodbye to his grandma and Colleen was in St. Louis at the time so she could see her grandma, too. Everyone had an opportunity to say goodbye to Alice, even Pat and Rose came from California. Within about a week, there was a funeral and party to send off Alice to heaven. She is still missed every single day. James live much longer but has now joined her in heaven, too. James went on to live in the same house all by himself. He was very sad and lonely but tried to stay busy and active so he could feel happier. James worked very hard on that and did a fine job. One day in nineteen ninety nine, James had a stroke and was in the hospital for a long time, about a month. When he got out of the hospital, he needed help so he went home with Mike and Janine. He stayed with them for about two months and then felt well enough to go home. He continued to stay in that house for a long time, until two thousand two or three. Then he moved to a retirement home and later to the Veteran's nursing home. They took really good care of James there and in the year two thousand eight, James passed away and joined Alice in heaven. He is missed every day, too.

Another important event that occurred was the wedding or Ryan Murphy and Meghan O'Connor in June of two thousand seven. James was still alive then and planning on attending the wedding but wasn't well enough to go. Ryan and Meghan visited James at the nursing home a few days later and he enjoyed that a lot. It is because Ryan and Meghan came together and got married that you two boys and your baby brother came to be. The family is better with you as part of it.

As a little more family history, Colleen married Mike Farrell in May of two thousand fifteen, about a week after Fergus was born.

The Treasure Box

It is my belief that everyone should have their very own treasure box, one in which to put very special and favorite things in, especially private things. Awards, letters, notes, small pieces of jewelry, a rock or shell, a concert ticket, a photo. Anything that has a special meaning to one.

One day when three boys were visiting their grandpa, they came across a treasure box. They weren't allowed in Grandpa's bedroom and usually, almost always, followed the rules at Grandpa's house.

It all started when Grandpa agreed to babysit his three grandsons for the day on a beautiful fall Saturday in November. This is the first time Grandpa babysat all three boys at the same time. He decided he may as well give it a try because he enjoyed spending time with his grandsons and he was glad to be of help. The boys came over about eight o'clock in the morning and had their backpacks with them. They showed Grandpa all their important belongings they had in their backpacks; extra set of clothes, pajamas possibly by mistake, some lego guys and pokeman, a writing book for Malachy, a stuffed animal for Rafferty. Fergus had extra clothes and diapers. There were also a few books packed for Grandpa to read to the boys.

.Grandpa took the boys outside to the back yard. He showed them all the plants, trees flowers, the patio and the creek in the far back. There was also a fenced in compost area. They seemed quite interested in the creek but that was off limits. There was zero negotiation about that because there was a treacherous bank leading to the creek and the boys were not big enough for that yet. Something else in Grandpa's yard that looked interesting was a shed or a little house. Grandpa built a little playhouse for his kids, Sean and Meghan when they were little. There was a roof, window and door; it was a very cute house. Grandpa used it as a shed now so the boys couldn't play in there either. But Grandpa said if they really like the house, he will empty it out for the next time they come over to play. They all agreed they would like that and seemed pretty happy about that prospect. They all had cereal for breakfast and orange juice. Grandpa also filled their water bottles for them to keep outside. At some point, Fergus would come inside for a nap, in a couple of hours. For now, they are finishing breakfast and ready to explore.

Malachy and Rafferty were very excited about being able to play in this beautiful and interesting back yard. It was different and fun. They had been here before but always with their mom and never just to play. This morning, Grandpa brought all the breakfast foods outside. Malachy helped him carry some of it and Rafferty watched Fergus. Grandpa brought his newspaper and coffee because while the boys were playing, he was going to ease into his morning, or so he thought. He might have forgotten that when you have three kids under six years of age, you don't ease into your day but you hit the ground running. Grandpa was optimistic about his coffee and paper.

He knew the boys would be there all day and wanted to pace himself, reserve some energy for later in the day. Good luck, Grandpa.

Into the yard they went, running, talking, playing, singing, having a blast. Fergus was too small to follow the big boys so Grandpa managed to keep him on the patio with some sidewalk chalk and other toys. He was pretty happy to be out there with the group. After a couple hours, Grandpa told Malachy and Rafferty he was going inside for a little while to change Fergus's diaper and put him down for a nap. He gave strict instructions again to stay away from the creek and if they needed him to come into the house and call his name. Grandpa was treated to a full diaper and worked his way through that. Then he put Fergus down in the pack and play for a nap. He turned on the baby monitor and took the remote outside so he could hear Fergus and supervise Malachy and Rafferty at the same time. All was going well outside. When he couldn't see the boys, he could hear them and knew they were safe. Every now and then, Grandpa called them up for some water.

But they had been playing hard all day and having the most fun outside in Grandpa's yard Grandpa made a maze out of haystacks and shrubbery in his backyard for the boys to play in and find their way out of. They loved this so much, even when they mastered finding their way out of the maze. They raced each other to see how fast they could get through the maze. Especially when they knew their way around in the maze, they enjoyed taking their baby brother, Fergus, with them. He was too young to find his way around but he liked being with his brothers and following them around outside. It was a positive experience for all of them.

Grandpa made lemonade and sandwiches for lunch and brought them outside for everyone so they could relax on the patio and have lunch. That was really nice but the boys had more exploring to do after lunch. While they were eating, Grandpa received a text from the boys' mom saying she wouldn't be picking them up until bedtime. She asked if Grandpa would make sure the boys ate dinner, took a bath and put their pajamas on before she picked them up. Grandpa never supervised the boys in the bath tub before and was a bit apprehensive about that, especially with the baby. Malachy and Rafferty assured Grandpa they knew what to do and would be very careful in the bath tub. Grandpa and the boys finished lunch and prayed for strength of the rest of the day. Grandpa went inside to get Fergus. Fergus got a clean diaper and then had lunch outside. Now he felt great and walked around in the grass for a long while. Malachy asked Grandpa for a shovel or small spade, two please. Grandpa didn't know why they wanted these tools but now was fairly tired and decided he was ok not knowing; it might even be better not to know. He got the tools and bought them out to the boys.

Malachy and Rafferty were busy with lots of talking but suddenly it got quiet. Grandpa called out to them and they answered but remained quiet. They were digging and digging. What happened is they saw a pile of dirt that was slightly raised up and were curious about it so they dug. Rafferty took a dig and they heard his shovel make contact with something hard, maybe a rock. Well they kept going and finally saw something in the dirt. It looked ie a piece of wood. They dug around it more and could tell it was a box. They dug under it and put their shovels down. Together, they each grabbed an end of the box and slowly pulled it up. Wow, this looked like a real find. It as a medium sized treasure box with a lock on it and it was locked. The wood was pretty but had a lot of dirt on it. Next, they asked Grandpa for some rags. He obliged. They took those rags and cleaned all the dirt off the treasure box. Now it was beautiful with the wood grain proudly surfacing. They carried this treasure to Grandpa, thinking he would be very excited about it but he looked a little troubled. When Grandpa saw the box, he had a funny look on his face; it wasn't a happy one. He wasn't angry, just surprised and unsettled.

Well, boys come here and sit down with Grandpa. I have something to tell you. Now they were even more curious. Grandpa told them that the box they found belonged to their Grandma Me. He buried it after she passed away; that's what she wanted. Grandma was very private and didn't want anyone looking in her treasure box. The boys wanted to know what was in the treasure box? Why didn't Grandma want anyone to see it? Grandpa did his best to explain this to the boys.

The treasure box is a box in which a person puts very special artifacts of people and events that are important to them. These artifacts can be photos, invitations, cards, letters, notes, jewelry. One could put a rock or shell from a beach, a sand dollar, a stick, a wedding invitation, whatever it is that is important to that person. Usually a lot of what is in the treasure box is private.

The boys wanted to know if Grandpa had a treasure box and he told they he did but it's private. He said they will each get their own treasure box soon and they can think about what they want to put inside the treasure box. Also, he said that usually one will put things in the treasure box and then when the box gets crowded, they will remove some things and make way for others. This means you are always evaluating what is important to you. If you are ten years old and your treasure box is full, you will have to do a lot of editing over the years to end up with exactly what you want to stay in your treasure box.

Grandpa said, "Boys, I am going to keep this treasure box here. I want you to go out and play for an hour and then we will go inside and have a little quiet time. Now, while you are playing, think about what you will put in your treasure box when you get it. We will talk about that at dinner later." Malachy and Rafferty jumped up with joy and said, "Yay!" They liked this idea of deciding what is important to them. Also, knowing they will be able to edit the treasure box as they grow, made them feel like they can change the contents whenever they want. They did nothing but chatter excitedly while waiting for dinner.

The Float

Maureen was starting to get accustomed to being a single parent. It had been close to a year now and she moved to a different city, her hometown, with her two young children, Colleen and Ryan. Everything was new: the house, the neighborhood, the school, the people. Colleen and Ryan were making friends in school and Maureen was making friends with some of the classmates' parents. There was also the new job, the very first teaching job ever. What kept everyone together was being so close to their Aunt Rose and Uncle Larry. They lived a few blocks away and helped make this life transition easier and more pleasant for everyone.

The summer Maureen and kids moved to St. Louis, Uncle Larry suggested we sign the kids up for soccer. This was a surprise for Maureen because she didn't know soccer was even played in elementary schools. But Aunt Rose said it would be a good way for kids to meet new friends before school starts. So they signed up.

Sure enough, before school even started, Colleen and Ryan met new friends while at soccer practice. Maureen met parents while waiting at practice. Parents actually have a lot of time to get to know each other while waiting at practice because they're on the sidelines either sitting in lawn chairs or walking around the side of field.

Soccer practice went on for weeks then school started and soccer games started every weekend. Soccer games were a Saturday morning ritual for much of the school year. The Saturday morning routine was to have breakfast at home, gear up for playing the game or watching, pack a lawn chair and dress in layers. Also bring coffee in a thermos. There were concession stands at the soccer games with plenty of coffee and hot chocolate but the hot drinks were served in styrofoam. Maureen didn't enjoy drinking out of styrofoam. There were various food items for sale as well. Sometimes a kid had multiple games on the same day or a family had multiple kids playing on the same day. If you were lucky, they were on the same field or complex of fields.

The same faces were there every week; it was a social event, one Maureen missed after her kids were in high school and finished with the soccer leagues. It was one of those things that became tiresome to some degree but created a void when it was finished.

Maureen made some friends at the soccer events. One friend, Fran, was also new to the school. She had three sons, Bobby, David and Chris. Bobby and David were in high school and Chris was one year younger than Ryan. But Chris was on Ryan's soccer team. The teams consisted of youths spanning a two year grade level grouping. Like me, Fran grew up in St. Louis but moved away when married. Also like me, Fran returned to St. Louis after her divorce; it happened to be the same time that I returned to St. Louis. We both found that all of our friends from high school days were married and living a different lifestyle than we were so that led to either losing touch with those folks or just a very increased distance. Living as a single parent is something one can't imagine unless they are experiencing it themselves.

As a single parent, all of one's resources, including one's own energy, are poured into the effort of raising their kids and maintaining a balanced and happy family. Maureen tried to provide for the children's needs so they wouldn't suffer from not having a present dad. That dad was not present throughout their lives, with few exceptions. It isn't really possible to fill that void. But every single parent I've ever met tries to do just that. It's a job that's physically demanding as well as emotionally demanding. Maureen and Fran had much in common that they instantly understood when they met and learned each other were single parents. That parent goes to every practice and game, drives carpool to school and social events, does all the shopping, cooks every meal, does all the laundry, gets the car serviced, cleans the house, takes care of the yard, and the list goes on. So in this case, these single parents formed a friendship and were able to enjoy some adult conversations and adult support while the kids were having fun. It was a good thing for all. We also found another single parent who we befriended, barb. She had two daughters; one of them was in Colleen's class. Often we did family activities together and it provided a lot of support for each other and was fun.

One day when Fran and I were watching a soccer game, we chatted about activities we enjoyed. I mentioned that I always loved to go camping but my ex husband didn't so we never went. We did go once on a canoe trip and it was lots of fun but that was only once and before we had kids. Fran said she loved to go camping, too and had a tent and a lot of camping equipment. We talked about going on a weekend. We selected a weekend, then decided on where to go. The plan was to go after work on Friday and stay two nights, leaving Sunday. Fran didn't get off work early enough to get there in the daylight on that weekend so she and her sons came Sat instead of Friday.

On Friday after school, the three of us packed the car. Colleen and Ryan were so excited about this trip; they had been camping with Uncle Mike once and really liked that so they knew this would be fun. This was my first time camping with me being the only responsible adult. So I was apprehensive about this daunting responsibility . Safety first, comfort next and fun third. Those were my priorities. We had a drive of about two hours and a map so we locked everything up and got in the car for take off. We had plenty of time to get there before dark so we were not rushed. It was very hot, in the high 90s so we hoped that being out in the country, the temperature would be lower. The temperature was a little lower but humidity was high and hot is hot.

We arrived at our campsite and first surveyed it for a good flat spot to set up the tent. We did just that. The tent is not complicated to set up but does require effort and patience, especially when it's very hot outside. We were pleased with how we set up the tent and went inside to unzip the windows and let some air circulate. Upon walking back out of the tent, I realized the door was placed directly in front of a patch of poison ivy. So we found a different place and moved the tent. We were very lucky that we didn't contract poison ivy. Now that the tent is up, we unloaded the remainder of the car = the clothes, toys, food and equipment. There was a cooking stove and coffeepot, cooler, food, utensils, dishes, tablecloth, rope and much more. Then we collected wood to make a fire later and hung the lantern on the tree.

By this time we were tired and super hot, also a little hungry. We thought it would be a good idea to cool off before doing anything else. We walked to the river, which was very close by. People were floating down the river, wading and generally hanging around. A lot of people floated by in large black intertubes I asked one of the campers what those were and where you get them. They told me they were the intertubular to tires used in very large trucks and the gas stations close by sell them for a low price. The camper said people like them because they hold up really well, the rubber is thick and hard to puncture.

We decided to get some of these tires for floating tomorrow. We got plenty, enough for Fran and her boys; obviously they would want some, too. The gas station attendant blew them up and we put them in our car and tied the rest on the roof. We stacked them up at the campsite for the next day. We just knew that was going to be a fun trip. We had never done anything like that and were excited just thinking about it.

We prepared some food for dinner and ate at the picnic table. Afterwards we talked about the next morning's plans. Then we gathered our ditty bags and walked up to the rest room facilities. After that, we walked back to camp and went inside the tent to our beds. It was still hot outside but had cooled down quite a bit. I remember looking at the clock and it was only nine o'clock; it felt much later. I was wide awake. I was laying awake and thinking to myself, "You took these kids camping by yourself and made it this far. It's going to workout. Tomorrow there will be another adult with you, and more kids, older kids." This was comforting. I listened while Colleen and Ryan gradually fell asleep. They had a very exciting day and were filled with excitement thinking about tomorrow. So many thoughts were going through my head on that night. Regret that I had to do this by myself, joy for making the kids so happy, confidence that I could do it by myself, fear that something would go wrong. I said prayers of thanks to God for making it all possible and prayers for continued safety. It was very calming for me to say prayers before going to sleep and in this case I went to bed before I was really ready so I needed extra time to relax and unwind before my body would fall asleep. I can't wait for morning to come.

Part II

The next morning, we all woke up at first light. The temperature was cooler, though still hot but we had gotten accustomed to it. Everybody headed to the rest room first, then there was the business of having breakfast. We made a small fire and cranked up and made coffee. I made pancakes and eggs for the kids. I knew it would be a very long day so I wanted to make sure they had a substantial breakfast. Whenever I eat pancakes, they stay with me for the whole day; I don't even get hungry again until nighttime. That's what I was going for. We ate at the picnic table and enjoyed the music made by the cicadas. There was the constant rhythm of the cricket like insects. They visit us once every thirteen years so we got lucky with this camping trip coinciding with their rare visit.

After we cleaned up the breakfast dishes, we decided to go exploring a little bit since Fran and her family wouldn't be there for several hours. We walked on some trails and down by the river. That's when we learned of the good place to put our inner tubes for floating. We walked back to the campsite and got our swim gear ready for floating, then put on sunscreen. That's when Fran pulled up, much earlier than expected. She said they packed everything up the night before and just got up, had a bite to eat and took off very early. They were excited to get to the campsite. Fran's two older sons put up their tent and then they unpacked their car. Fran was known to travel with lots of stuff to make camping more comfortable. One thing Fran brought was a large tarp to put over a very large area in case it rained. This was very helpful because sometimes it did rain and instead of sitting in the tent to stay dry, we could stand or sit under this huge tarp. It also covered the picnic table and kept the food and equipment from getting wet. We found this very helpful. Also, there were times when we hung up towels and wet swimming suits to dry and put wet shoes by the fire to dry and wanted to keep the firewood dry. Again, this tarp was helpful, not to mention helpful for staying out of the direct sun, too. Fran also had some cool flashlights that stood up like lanterns, and some super comfortable lawn chairs. Unpacking and setting up camp was fairly quick for Fran and family because they had an extra set of hands. And Fran's two older boys were almost like grown ups in a way. They helped a lot.

When they finished, we all sat around the picnic table, which was now two picnic tables put together. We told them all about the floating and showed them the inner tubes. They were very excited. So we took a short walk to show them the place to put in the inner tubes. It was decided everyone wanted to go so we went back to the camp site. First we all got dressed in our swim suits with shirts for sun protection. Then we started to assemble food and drinks for lunch. We had fruit and made sandwiches. We even brought soda and bottled water. Next topic of discussion was how we planned to carry the cooler with us. No problem I said, because we can take some rope and create a web around the inside of the inner tube, and put the cooler there. That took a little trial and error to get the webbing just right, but we managed. We tied that webbed inner tube to another inner tube and then tied a lot of them together. We had extra rope in case we wanted to change the configuration of the tied inner tubes. And we did later so that was a good plan. We learned that we didn't all want to be right on top of each other for floating. Some areas of the river were narrow and our tied up version of inner tubes continued to get stuck on occasion. We still tied up with each other but didn't tie more than three together at a time. It was smoother and probably safer, too. With everything ready, we all walked down to the river together and got in the water. Off we went, floating.

It took a very short time to figure out the most comfortable position in which to float. For most people, it was, butt in the water, knees over one end of the inner tube and arms, shoulders and head over the other end. Sometimes it was fun to just hang on with arms, having the rest of your body in the water. We didn't get at all hot the rest of this day; the water kept us cooled off nicely. We started floating down the river at a nice clip. Others were out on this beautiful day, too. Many were in canoes, others in rafts and lots of folks in inner tubes.

For me, I had never in my life felt such an incredible sense of relaxation. The experience was so pleasant. I only needed to keep the sun out of my eyes with a hat, which required repositioning the hat once in awhile. Then there was the bouncing off of random logs or other inner tubes. Otherwise, nothing much required of me. The stress of planning the trip and going camping without another adult; it all melted away in the most delightful manner. I imagine if a masseuse gave me a massage after the float, he or she would have noted how relaxed my muscles already were. That was quite a change from my normal tightened up muscles.

Hours went by and it was like a dream come true. When people were thirsty, they floated over to the cooler and got a drink. There was no hassle. Nobody had any problems and there were no squabbles. We all stopped and got out of the inner tubes at a sand bar and had lunch. We also took a break there for a while. A break from what? Ha ha. Such delight. I could have floated like that for days.

We saw many interesting things along this float. From on top of the water, you can't tell the difference between a snake's head and a turtle's head; of course we pretended like they were all turtles. And we did see a few turtles along the way, most of them hanging out on a log in the river. The banks of the river were all different depths with plenty of tree roots exposed. Some waters were deep and cold, some were shallow and clear. In some areas, the water was very shallow and created ripples. In those areas, we had to stand up and walk across to deeper water, or our butts would be ripped up with gravel.

All along the river, we were thrilled with this experience but after about five hours of floating, one person said, "Hey, how are we going to get back to the campsite?" Wow. What a good question, an appropriate question and asked not by an adult but by a kid. Fran and I laughed so hard because we were having such a great time and were so relaxed, we forgot to factor that into our plan. We were both in the single parent mode where we were the only ones planning and making decisions all the time. This was just a strange fluke that we missed the boat on it.

So as we continued to float down the river, we decided to ask fellow floaters, strangers, how they get themselves back to their cars or campsites. Well some of them were on a group float and would be picked up by a bus and others arranged to have an extra car at the end of the float so they could drive back to their camp spot. We floated many miles on the river, and it was many more by car. So we thought about this for a while as we continued to float. We knew we couldn't all gather up our inner tubes and walk back to camp. Fran decided we needed to hitch hike. Hitch hike on the river. Her thinking was that most of the people were probably campers and returning to the same place we were. We had seven people. Nobody would have room for seven people. We decided Fran would hitchhike and get her car. Then she would drive back and pick up the rest of us. Except, her car might not fit all seven of us and our inner tubes. So maybe we could send Fran and two kids while I remain with the rest of them. We agreed this could work. We need only to find that person who will give us a ride . Still we float and float.

Finally we see an older couple who were floating on a really big air mattress. We struck up a conversation with them, telling them of our dilemma. They offered to give us a ride and said they were getting out of the water up ahead a little way. We followed them to the place where we got out.

Everyone got out and stretched. Fran, Chris and Ryan went with the couple in their car to the campsite. Fran returned by herself in her own car about an hour later. We were so happy to see her. By that time, we all wanted a shower and dry clothes. First we loaded the inner tubes into the trunk of the car and tied the rest on top of the roof. Then we returned to the campsite wet, tired and hungry. We all took showers and got dry clothes on. After that we rooted around for what we could have for dinner. It turns out Fran and I precooked dinner, frozen it, and now just have to thaw it out. Chili it would be. I made the chili and Fran made a chocolate cake. That was the best meal we ever ate.

First Time Camping

Maureen and her two kids, Colleen and Ryan, planned to visit Maureen's brother, Mike on the weekend. Maureen figured it might be a seven hour drive so they would leave immediately after school on Friday. Mike lived outside of Bloomington, Indiana and Maureen lived in St. Louis, Missouri. During the planning, Maureen checked google maps and determined the drive was only about four hours; that is good news. Still, leaving home immediately after school on a Friday is the plan we are going to stick with. Mike is Maureen's older brother by seventeen months. He is single and Maureen hasn't been to his place yet. She and the kids are looking forward to it.

Maureen told Colleen and Ryan to pack clothes for a variety of temperatures. Since it was fall, we couldn't predict the weather. At this point we didn't plan on camping but instead planned on staying in Uncle Mike's A Frame cottage at the edge of the woods. We packed our little tent just in case there wasn't enough room but we didn't expect to use it. We packed the tent, a cooler and the rest was clothes to wear. There was no packing of camping gear other than the tent.

Maureen returned home from work about three thirty and the kids had the tent, cooler and their bags in the car before she could change her clothes. We wanted to get on the road, drive for about two hours and then stop to eat, if it wasn't too crowded. Mike expected us between eight and nine o'clock; it would be dark when we arrived. At his place, there were no street lights and it's hard to find in the dark but it wasn't possible for me to leave any earlier so we would figure it out. Also, this was around the year nineteen eighty three, pre cell phones; so it was important to stick as closely to the schedule as possible otherwise I would have to search for someplace to stop and find a pay phone along the way.

Off we went on our little weekend road trip. We listened to some stories on the radio as we traveled. About half way through, we stopped at a Denny's for a meal. Denny's is a place I haven't visited in about twenty years. Back then it seemed like a reasonably priced place to go with two kids. Also, one knew what one was getting when the went to denny's regardless of the city. After a meal and a rest room visit, we returned to the car and continued our trip to Uncle Mike's house at the edge of the woods.

We arrived at Uncle Mike's house about eight thirty in the evening. He was waiting for us and was prepared to go out and try to find us is we got lost. Fortunately we made it. Colleen and Ryan liked Uncle Mike's place a lot. He had a loft with his bedroom on top. The way to get up there was a ladder; that certainly was a lot different from the traditional fed on the floor in a room. The place was very cute. The view out the front windows was of Brown County National Forest; all one could see was trees. It was a beautiful view. That night we went to bed about ten pm because we planned to do some hiking and boating the next day.

Saturday morning we had breakfast with Uncle Mike at his place. Then he asked if we wanted to go camping in the woods. Well I told Mike that we did bring our tents but didn't bring any other camping equipment with us. He said he had equipment and didn't have a tent but he would sleep out doors. We thought that sounded like fun so we said we would go.

We drove to a good camp spot in Brown County National Park. The campsite was close to a lady and some trails so it was perfect. Colleen and Ryan thought it was great fun to pump water out of a spigot via an old fashioned handle pump. They fetched water to heat up over the fire. We all went out on a walk looking for kindling and logs to make a fire. We did get a good fire going and that was a good thing because it was a little chilly outside.

Mike and I used the hot water to make some coffee. We heated up canned stew for lunch and again the kids thought that was a lot of fun, they said it was just like the cowboys. Getting water from the pump and heating up canned stew was just like the cowboys.

We went out for a boat ride in a row boat and enjoyed that quite a bit. Unlike in Missouri's, this time we weren't getting into the water when taking out a boat. It was far too cold. The experience was quite different. In the afternoon, the kids played on the playground, which was near the camp site. Later, when it was time for bed, we had our first camping experience in which we spent the night. It was a lot of fun. The kids wanted to tell ghost stories in the tent when it was dark outside

There's nothing quite like the outdoors. Waking up in the morning to the fresh air is most delightful. We had a fun trip with Uncle Mike and now we're ready for our journey home.

A Missing Child, Temporarily

Long ago there was a family with a mom, dad, two boys and two girls. The oldest child was ten and the youngest child was two. The child who came up missing for a while was three years old.

The dad worked for a big company as a mechanical engineer. The mom worked as a mom for four kids. She took care of the needs of everyone in the family and the house.

The mom and dad shared one car. The year was nineteen fifty six. In the year nineteen fifty six, most middle class families lived in a house with only one bathroom and they were a middle class family living in an eleven thousand dollar house. Children shared bedrooms. And the car. How did they manage? In this case, if the mom wanted or needed the car for the day, she had to get all four kids in the car and take the dad to work then drive back home again and start the breakfast routine. But the dad joined a carpool. Back in the nineteen fifties, car pools were quite common because there was a need for them. Today car pools are becoming more popular because people are concerned about conserving energy. Back to the dad. The dad was in the car pool which freed up the car four days a week. That was plenty of days for the mom to use the car since the kids all were either with her or walked to school. Her visiting and errands could be done on those four days when the dad was a passenger in the car pool. The dad tended to run late every single day and the car pool people were in the driveway honking. Through the years, the dad got kicked out of the car pool occasionally for being late or staying too late at work at the end of the work day. One thing the dad did that was funny is this; because he was running late but still wanted his coffee, he poured the coffee into a saucer to cool off and continued getting dressed. When dressed and ready to go, he leaned over the sink with the saucer and carefully drank the coffee so as not to get any on his shirt or tie. What most people do today if they are running late and want some coffee, is to pour it in a travel mug and take it with them. In fact, most people today travel with water bottles, the insulated type and / or coffee travel mugs or thermoses. So in nineteen fifty six, the car pool was coffee and water free.

In this family's house there were three bedrooms and six people. The mom and dad slept in one bedroom, the two boys slept in another bedroom and the two girls slept in another bedroom. If overnight guests visited from another state, some of the kids slept on the floor while the guests had their beds. The kids not only didn't mind this, but approached it as a fun adventure. The adventure involved sleeping in a different room or possibly staying up a little later; it was fun.

The house had plenty of room for the family but wasn't big, approximately eight hundred square feet. Christmas and Easter celebrations were held there with lots of extended family and everyone made the most of the space available. It was the norm at that time. In two thousand sixteen, it seems people prefer larger houses or at least more open floor plans to maximize the space. That house on Estridge is likely a starter home for someone now. The basement was great because there was a cement floor and we roller skated there in the winter. We also had a piano downstairs, which must have been quite a challenge to get down the stairs. Some years we even decorated a second Christmas tree down there. It seems the floor was tiled at some point.

The mom and dad did not go out often without kids. Sometimes they did go out and leave the kids with a grandma type babysitter. They felt safe and comfortable with her and she came repeatedly. Back in those days, babysitters charged about twenty five cents an hour. Keep in mind the medium income levels to determine how cheap it was, likely not as cheap as it sounds today. Mom and dad were probably going to a friend's house for a bridge party; they did this once a month. When it was their turn to host, no babysitter was needed.

While mom and dad were gone, the kids played for a while and then got ready for bed. This time, the baby sitter was a teen aged girl from down the street. Everything seemed ok; the girl was pleasant and nothing unusual happened. The kids were fairly well behaved and cooperative, Everybody went to bed as expected, probably around eight oclock. It's not clear what the babysitter did after the kids went to bed. She could have been doing homework, reading, maybe talking on the phone to a friend. The phone wasn't as likely because there were party lines at that time and one couldn't just hang on the phone and talk endlessly. Someone from another house would need to make a phone call and everybody had to share. The community members had to share with each other; that was a very different time.

Mom and dad came home, not terribly late but around ten or eleven at night. They chatted with the baby sitter for a few minutes and then checked on the kids in their room. This was standard procedure before the dad drove the babysitter home. During the bedroom check, one kid was missing - not in his bed. It was Patrick; he was known to be a night roamer but was usually found in the bedroom or living room. The mom and dad asked the babysitter questions about what happened and she relayed the events of the evening simply as she knew them. She was not aware that any child got up from his or her bed and walked away. As previously described, the house is very small; it's difficult to imagine anyone could leave without being noticed. The front door was in the living room. There was a back door through the kitchen. If the baby sitter was in the dining room, she may not have seen a person walk past the opening behind her. However, it is her responsibility to make sure everyone is safe and to check on them periodically. Apparently this did not happen.

Panic struck the mom and dad; they woke up the two older kids to ask questions and the dad took the babysitter home. The boy and girl didn't know what happened; as far as they knew, everyone went to bed and nobody put up a fuss. They started searching under beds, in closets, the basement, behind the couch, under the table, behind the shower curtain - no Patrick. Now it wasn't likely that anyone kidnapped the little boy so they decided he must have walked out the back door. Outside they went

-also in the garage - around the house, throughout the backyard and front yard - no Patrick. The dad returned from dropping off the babysitter and joined the search in the back yard. It was spring time in Missouri, a little crisp outside but not so cold that you would be miserable without proper attire. After everyplace was searched, the mom, dad and two kids were on the patio in the dark and one of them said, "Hey, what about the dog house? Did anyone check the dog house?" No one had checked it yet but that is exactly where they found Patrick, sound asleep on the floor of the dog house. The dog was in the people, comfortable on the couch. This dog house was nice, built recently by the kids' grandfather. It was well constructed with a shingled roof, windows and shutters. No heat in the house but it did have insulation and a nice wooden floor.

Patrick was now awake and curious as to what was going on. When asked why he was out there, he didn't really know. He may have thought it would be fun or he may have been sleep walking and not know exactly it all happened. But everyone was happy and relieved to find him and went inside to check on the other two kids again. To this day, Patrick sleep walks. One day his wife found him with his car keys in his hands and walking out to his car at about three in the morning. She said, "Patrick, wake up," several times and he did. She asked where he was going and he said to work. But it was about three and a half hours too early for that. He went back to bed then, too.

Sleep tight.

www.ingramcontent.com/pod-product-compliance
Lightning Source LLC
Chambersburg PA
CBHW041011170626
46815CB00003B/258